"What will it feel like, Harri? How will we know when it's happening?" Payton asked, as breathless as she.

"What?" Her voice was a panting whisper; her heart an erratic pounding in her ears; her body spiraling with excitement and expectation.

"The magic," he murmured, his breath warm against her lips. "How will we know when it's taking effect? What will it feel like?"

"I don't know," she answered, mesmerized by sensation.

Hot and panting, she felt him setting stray wisps of curling hair away from her face with a tender touch. She opened her eyes to see the amazement, the passion, and the longing that were clouding her own mind. "We shouldn't do this," she said with a gasp, wishing she had one good reason not to.

"Too late," he told her. "We already are . . . ."

WHAT ARE *LOVESWEPT* ROMANCES?

They are stories of true romance and touching emotion. We believe those two very important ingredients are constants in our highly sensual and very believable stories in the *LOVESWEPT* line. Our goal is to give you, the reader, stories of consistently high quality that may sometimes make you laugh, sometimes make you cry, but are always fresh and creative and contain many delightful surprises within their pages.

Most romance fans read an enormous number of books. Those they truly love, they keep. Others may be traded with friends and soon forgotten. We hope that each *LOVESWEPT* romance will be a treasure—a "keeper." We will always try to publish

*LOVE STORIES YOU'LL NEVER FORGET
BY AUTHORS YOU'LL ALWAYS REMEMBER*

The Editors

®
611

Mary Kay McComas

THE TROUBLE WITH MAGIC

®

BANTAM BOOKS

NEW YORK · TORONTO · LONDON · SYDNEY · AUCKLAND

THE TROUBLE WITH MAGIC

A Bantam Book / April 1993

If you would be interested in receiving protective vinyl
covers for your Loveswept books, please write to this address
for information:

Loveswept
Bantam Books
P.O. Box 985
Hicksville, NY 11802

ISBN 0-553-44378-X

Published simultaneously in the United States and Canada

PRINTED IN THE UNITED STATES OF AMERICA

OPM   0 9 8 7 6 5 4 3 2 1

For Matt and Nick and Ben.
It's okay to believe in miracles.
Your mom says so, and she has you as proof.

One

He was a man who had no problems with the world. He didn't miss anything he didn't miss anything he didn't already own, and there was no one in his life he couldn't walk away from. So, what was he doing in the sleepy river town of St. Peter's Bay?

He shook his head as he surveyed the lethargic little community with a jaded eye. It was that woman, and those cursed letters, and all the phone calls that had compelled him to come. Forced him to come. He didn't like being *forced* into doing anything.

He stood in the portico of the picturesque hotel and watched the long black limousine drive away. He had a distinct impression that he should be going with it. Slipping a hand into the pocket of his tailor-made slacks, he turned his attention to the small marina.

Changes would have to be made. He'd expected as much when his investment broker had suggested an interest in one of the Thousand Islands of the St. Lawrence River, specifically Jovette Island. But he hadn't anticipated the town being quite so . . . so . . . banal. Granted, it was November, a bit off-season.

Luckily, he was a man of vision. He also had the

resources and the know-how to turn the slumbering village into a thriving commercial enterprise.

But first he'd have to deal with Harriet Wheaton, and her damnable letters, and her constant interference.

Stepping inside the hotel, he noted the decor. There was a definite nautical theme to it. But rather than the usual fishnet and oars, the place was an antique dealer's dream of seafaring memorabilia—lanterns, compasses, depth finders, cabin trunks, ships in bottles, portraits. . . .

"May I help you, sir?" the desk clerk asked.

"Payton Dunsmore," he said, still taking inventory.

"This is the gentleman I made the reservation for, Cyrus," a female voice said from directly behind him—a distinctly familiar female voice. He turned his head. "I'm Harriet Wheaton, Mr. Dunsmore."

Harriet Wheaton. He took her hand and shook it, amazed that she wasn't at all what he had expected.

She was young. Maybe not yet thirty. Her dark hair was pulled back from her face as if she had nothing to hide, her skin had a healthy glow.

Big dark eyes watched him from behind a pair of tortoise shell glasses that gave her the appearance of being thoughtful and sensuous rather than studious and clinical. Her gaze was direct and inquisitive—not unlike his own.

"Ms. Wheaton," he said automatically. It was on the tip of his tongue to tell her it was a pleasure to see her. Not to meet her, of course. So far the woman had proved to be nothing but a pain in the posterior. But looking at her was indeed a pleasure, though he wasn't sure why.

She wasn't beautiful, not even remarkably pretty. Her eyes were too big and so were the glasses, and they made her nose look too small for her face. She had an engaging smile; her teeth were straight and even, but there was a slight crookedness to her mouth that kept drawing his attention. She was dressed in blue jeans, sneakers, a bulky knit sweater, and a slicker. Although her body was nondescript, he had the sudden urge to touch her.

Maybe it was the little tendrils of hair that had escaped their bonds and lay curled against her cheek that were driving him crazy. If he could just smooth them back, very gently . . .

"You didn't have any trouble getting here, did you?" she asked, watching him closely, curiously.

"No. Not at all," he said. He squared his shoulders and reminded himself that he wasn't happy with the woman. "The chauffeur you sent seemed to know where he was going."

"Oh. Yes, of course, he would. I'm sorry I asked you here so late in the season," she said, restarting her polite conversation while she lost a pound of water through the palms of her hands. Lord, she was nervous. "Being from Tampa, you might have enjoyed seeing upstate New York in the summertime. And I'm afraid you've missed our beautiful fall foliage as well."

"I'm familiar with the seasons in this part of the country, Ms. Wheaton. Lovely as they are, however, I didn't come here for the scenery."

Her brows rose, but only the ends closest to the bridge of her nose. Being a good bad guy wasn't going to be easy.

"No. Of course not," she said, rejecting small talk. Rejecting many of her preconceived notions about him at the same time.

It was disconcerting to realize that she had forgotten one of the fundamental rules of research. There is a vast distinction between studying a phenomenon and experiencing it. Payton Dunsmore was a phenomenon that needed to be experienced. He was more . . . much, much more than she had anticipated.

"Had you planned to go up to your room first or would you simply prefer to get on with it?" she asked, her throat tightening as she took in the tall, well-developed man before her.

Knowing he had a thirty-seven-inch inseam, a thirty-five-inch waist, and a size seventeen-and-a-half collar, she still wasn't prepared for the sight of him.

He glanced at the desk clerk.

"I'm sure the room is fine," he said with a nod. "If I could leave my bag here, I'll check in later."

"The room's been taken care of, sir. I can have your bag taken up, if you like," the man offered, shifting his eyes from Payton to Harriet and back, unsure of whom to take his directions from—Harriet, who was running the show, or Payton, the special guest star.

"That'll be fine," she said, and then passing a slip of paper across the desk to him, she added, "And could you fax this for me when you get a minute? There won't be a reply."

"Sure, Harri," he said with strained familiarity. He smiled limply and nodded. He then went about his business, unaware of the crime in progress and his participation in it.

Harriet sighed, battling the regret and disappointment she was growing accustomed to now that so many of her old friends found it hard to look her in the eye. She turned her attention back to Payton.

"Are you sure you wouldn't like to change your clothes?" she asked, eyeing his expensive suit. "It's a nice sunny day, but it's cold out, and it'll be colder out on the water. You can only get to the island by boat, you know."

"I believe that's common to most islands," he said with a dry expression.

She gave a little laugh and felt like an idiot. To redeem herself, she said, "I'm sure you know, though, that several of the bigger islands are connected to the mainland by bridges."

She could see he was dying to say something.

"What?" she asked.

He smiled. There was a spark of humor in his mossy green eyes.

"I'm just surprised that you're nervous," he said, stepping around her toward the door, disinclined to change his attire. "I'd have sworn you didn't have a nerve in your body."

"Why?" It would have done no good to deny his observation. She was a criminal, but she was lousy at it.

"The letters. The phone calls. The little wrenches you keep throwing into this deal. You didn't give me the impression that you were particularly concerned about being a nuisance."

"I wasn't. But why would that make me nerve*less*?" she asked, irritated, aware that she was splitting hairs but unable to stop herself. He held the door open for her. "Why couldn't it be a matter of having too much nerve?"

He looked at her in such a way that she felt obliged to explain.

"Well, nerveless makes me sound like some fool who's blundering her way through this mess. I know what I'm doing, Mr. Dunsmore. Every letter, every phone call, every wrench was a deliberate act in my attempt to save my island," she said, her anger fading to an irate curiosity. She stepped onto the dock and then turned to face him. "Why nerveless? Why couldn't you have thought I was incredibly nerv*y*?"

He pondered this, watching the loose wisps of hair around her face as they fluttered in the wind. Actually, he did think her nervy. Also presumptuous, pushy, and more than a little pigheaded, but he sensed that it wasn't his minor grammatical error she was reacting to, it was something else. She wasn't scolding him, she was asking a question of the world in general. He was intrigued.

"You're right, of course. Linguistically, I stand corrected," he said diplomatically. "But why would you care what I, or anyone else, thought of you? As you say, you're an intelligent woman who knows what she's doing. It shouldn't matter what I think of you."

"It shouldn't . . ." she admitted, knowing she'd overreacted. " . . . but it does. What you think colors the attitude you take toward people, toward me."

The attitude he took toward people was always the same—he took them for all they had. He'd take her, too, eventually. With relish and onions. And he'd enjoy it, for not many people were unwise enough to cross him the way she had. In the meantime, he thought benevolently, it wouldn't hurt to let her talk.

"I can assure you, Ms. Wheaton, that my attitude toward you would have been the same whether I thought you nerveless or nerv*y*," he said quite honestly.

She liked watching his mouth when he talked. He had nice teeth, and his lips were almost too perfectly shaped.

She nodded, and they walked on in thoughtful silence.

With the passing of summer, life around St. Peter's Bay settled like slow-falling leaves until only a thin layer of tourists covered the tightly knit core of the river community, small-town people who spent half their lives catering to the whims of others, and the other half trying to make ends meet.

Harriet was part of that core. Her life wasn't structured for tourism, but there had been a Jovette on Jovette Island since before St. Peter's Bay was St. Peter's Bay; since before the canals; since before there was a boundary between Canada and the United States—and it wasn't going to change now. Not if Harriet could help it.

Criminally speaking, however, she wasn't concerned with who saw her on the docks with Payton Dunsmore. The tourists wouldn't remember them two seconds after eye contact, and the locals wouldn't think twice about her sailing a guest out to the island. They all knew the situation she was in, but none of the specifics. They knew, too, that she hadn't winterized the island and returned to the city yet. She'd picked Thanksgiving week for her crime for several reasons, but primarily to dampen any curiosity that might arise. All in all, she felt her plan to be quite solid.

Payton sighed.

If Harriet Wheaton thought she was pulling any new tricks on him, she had at least one more good think coming to her. He knew all about her. Granted, he'd been a little surprised to discover that she was so appealing, but it hadn't been relevant, and it didn't change the facts.

She was unemployed. She'd been in jail for the better part of the past two years for a crime involving some sort of deception at a chemical plant. And surprise, surprise, she was about to attempt the oldest, dirtiest trick in the book of real estate on him! The old my-property-is-a-run-down-pile-of-rotten-wood with-holes-in-the-roof-and-a-leaky-cellar-and-you-don't-really-want-it trick. Truthfully, he'd expected better of her. He'd hoped that perhaps someone who'd been to prison might be more imaginative in their subterfuge.

On the other hand, he thought with a wily smile, it might prove entertaining to allow Ms. Wheaton all the rope she needed to entangle herself. Once snared and as helpless as a trapped animal, he might kiss her. Once. To satisfy his curiosity; to know for sure if her mouth was as sweet and provocative as it looked; if her skin was as soft. . . .

And then, of course, he'd snatch her island out from under her, just as he'd planned.

"Do you sail, Mr. Dunsmore?" she asked, stopping beside a small skiff.

Did he sail? Payton's eyes shifted from the dinghy bobbing dockside to Harriet's face. Was she kidding? Of course, he'd sailed before—he lived in Tampa for crissake! But it wasn't his favorite form of transportation. He had a landlubber's soul and preferred to be in contact with solid ground at all times. But, be that as it may, on the occasions when water jaunts couldn't be avoided, he generally consumed a fistful of motion-sickness pills and always, *always* made sure the vessel was considerably bigger than his Uncle Farnsworth's shoe!

His gaze darted to the vast expanse of choppy, fitful water before him and then back to the catboat.

"Ships sail, Ms. Wheaton," he said. "I doubt this toy would get fifty feet out before it capsized."

"It's perfectly safe," she assured him with a smile. "I came across this morning in it. Truly."

"Yes, well, if I'd realized that you were planning an adventure for this afternoon, I would have taken your suggestion to change my clothes. As it is, I'd rather not spend the rest of the day drenched to the bone. Perhaps there's something else available. . . ." he said, looking around, leaving little doubt as to whether he was making a request or delivering an imperative to change boats.

She turned, and he followed her wistful gaze to an exquisite thirty-foot yawl in a slip across the way.

"Yes. That's more like it," he said, much relieved.

She laughed softly. "Well, at least you know beautiful when you see it," she said, bending to cast off the dinghy.

"Can't you sail a boat that size?" he asked, frowning as the line slipped from the mooring ring. He rubbed the dimenhydrinate patch at the base of his neck and wished he had applied two. It was a precaution he'd taken earlier, knowing that where there was an island, there was also water and that inevitably he'd be crossing it. "My experience is limited but if you refresh my memory, I think I could be a pretty good first mate."

She moved to the second line without comment.

"Think of it, Ms. Wheaton," he said, coaxing her. "You'd be in the enviable position of giving me orders for however long it takes us to get to the island and back. I have employees who'd give their right arms for an opportunity like this."

She looked up and was greeted with a wide, teasing grin that tickled her insides into knots. She laughed.

"I admit it's tempting, Mr. Dunsmore. I knew I'd live to regret selling that boat."

"You sold it?"

"I have debts to pay," she said simply.

He glanced back at the yawl with its polished brass fittings and glossy planking. Its name, *Enchantment*, was proudly painted in brilliant white across the transom. One couldn't be Payton Dunsmore IV for thirty-six years without developing an acute sense of material worth somewhere along the way. He knew a prized treasure when he saw one, and he intuitively knew the price she'd paid to sell it.

"Maybe we could rent it for the afternoon," he said, thinking it would be a treat for her, as well as his salvation.

"Would you rent out a boat like that?" she asked, sure of his answer.

He looked to the yawl and then back at the catboat. He loathed the idea of exposing his fears to the woman, giving her an upper hand. He'd rather die than show her any weakness—and very likely would if he didn't. He opened his mouth to speak and closed it again.

"Trust me, Mr. Dunsmore. I'll take you out to the island, safe and sound, and I won't even get your shoes wet."

She was smiling that beguiling little lopsided smile, and the crazy little curls about her face were whipping innocently in the wind. The glasses and her big dark eyes fairly screamed of her dependability and trustworthiness. He knew better than to rely on her, but . . .

"I want a life jacket," he said.

She smiled at him and sighed with relief.

TWO

Payton Dunsmore wasn't as ignorant of sailing as he'd led her to believe, she noticed quickly. They sailed at a close reach, across the wind at a right angle. Instinctively, he felt the change in the wind, knew when to bow to the boom and when to shift his weight for balance. He watched her closely for a while before visibly beginning to relax and seeming almost to enjoy the ride. Almost.

She lowered her gaze, too amused to look at him. Were his earlier qualms due to the size of the dinghy? Or because her sailing skills were an unknown to him? Or to the simple fact that he was about to lose control of the situation?

She had a feeling that Payton Dunsmore was a man who made a point of always being in control—of his business, of his life, of his emotions. Part of her giggled while the rest of her shuddered to think of his reaction when he discovered exactly how much control he'd relinquished to her when he'd stepped into her boat.

An affable silence settled over them. Both were introspective; both were aware of the other—though Payton's attention was divided by the profuse amount of water and the way it rolled and pitched and tossed the tiny boat. Harriet would direct his attention to prominent points of interest and relate a bit of the history of each. He would nod and take note.

It was a piece of good fortune that he was better looking—more human looking than he'd looked in his pictures, she mused, admiring his strong profile as he watched Cedar Island growing small in the distance behind them. If push came to shove, and she was forced to carry out her plan, his good looks were going to make everything so much easier.

She liked his thick dark hair. And she liked that he was due for a haircut. A small riot of curls behind his ears was in dire need of being clipped back into perfection—to match the impeccable fit of his suit and the shine of his shoes. She was warming to the idea that he wasn't the immaculate, flawless man he appeared to be.

A wave broke and a sudden gust of wind sent a spray of water into his face. She shrugged and grimaced apologetically. He was oblivious to the smile he sent her in return.

It wasn't half bad, sailing open waters in something the size of a standard bathtub. As a matter of fact, the ride was so smooth that if he didn't think about it, he could think of other things.

For example, he couldn't get over his impression that she was perhaps the most beautiful woman he'd ever come across. It was ludicrous. His women were generally of the ravishing variety—strikingly attractive faces, luscious bodies, benign personalities. The nicest thing he could say about Harriet Wheaton was that she was a troublemaker with an ordinary body and an interesting face.

Still, his fingers were itching to touch her. When their eyes met there was a peculiar clutching in his belly that he couldn't remember experiencing since his high school days. There was even a strange euphoric sensation in his chest when he'd catch glimpses of her with the wind in her face and the excitement of sailing in her dark, dark eyes. It was very queer.

"Jovette Island is up ahead there," she called to him over the sound of rushing wind and lapping waves. He turned to look. "When we're close enough, we'll come about to get a better view of the house."

The island was almost a mile long at its furthest points and forty acres at its widest. Like most of the other one thousand eight hundred-odd islands in the strait, its slopes were thickly quilled with pines and hardwoods. And along with so many of its neighbors, it had become part of a playground for the rich in the late eighteen hundreds.

Payton had all the data. Jovette Island boasted a soaring Victorian manor with twenty-three rooms, eight bathrooms, jutting towers and turrets, a veranda and a gazebo. But its history went back further than the house's architecture for it also had a small log cabin preserved on the northeastern, the Canadian, side of the island.

The house had a two-color slate roof and was dark olive-green, trimmed in gold and terra-cotta on the bargeboards, scalloped friezes, and porch brackets, with just a touch of Indian red here and there for accent.

"Those are the original colors, aren't they?" he asked, turning to look at her with some degree of respect.

He was certainly no authority, but somewhere along the way, he'd heard that most Victorian homes had been painted white in later years to impress people with their unique lines and size. However, true Victorians, were not only colorful in their thinking and in their life styles, but also in the tints they applied to their homes.

"Yes, they are," she called back, equally impressed with his knowledge of Victorian architecture. He had nice hands, too, she noticed distractedly. Big hands. If he were to touch a woman with those hands, the woman would know it, from the roots of her hair to her toenails, she'd know it. "My father did it," she said abruptly.

"What?"

"The house was white once," she said. Making a sweeping gesture with her hand, she added, "Like all the others. But my father was a bit of an amateur historian. And of course he came to love the house, so he restored it after my mother died. People said he was crazy to paint it those colors, but I love it."

"Why after your mother died? Wouldn't she have approved?"

She shrugged. "I'm not sure. I always thought it was more a matter of not wanting to hurt her feelings by changing too many things on the island. . . . It was her island, you see. Then it was mine."

"Not your father's?"

"He wasn't a Jovette."

"Neither are you."

She laughed. "It's a blood thing. My ancestors were French," she shouted over the wind and water, grinning. "Blood's very important to the French, you know."

"Well, I do now," he said, shaking his head and turning back to look at the house, revamping it in his mind.

With no little skill, she maneuvered the tiny boat into irons, into the wind, several boat lengths from the dock and let the wind act as a brake, bringing it to a standstill close to the mooring rings. He jumped out while she brought the sail down and then tossed him a line.

"So? Are your shoes wet?" she asked, coming to stand next to him on the dock. They both looked down at his still shiny—and still dry—shoes. "I'm glad I didn't say anything about your hair or your jacket."

He looked up into her eyes and felt the clutching in his abdomen again. He knew an overpowering urge to reach out, grab her into his arms, and kiss the smirk off her face—and then he wanted to slap himself back to his senses. Was he losing his mind?

"They're not too bad," he admitted, checking both jacket and hair with one hand. Then, feeling incredibly magnanimous, he added, "You're a fine sailor."

"Thank you," she said, pleased by his praise.

They stood on the dock, staring hard at each other for a long moment before an awkwardness set in and they looked off in different directions.

"I . . . I suppose we could start the tour here," she said, pointing. "The boat house has three slips. It's weather tight. The roof was new four years ago."

"What about this dock?" he asked.

She shrugged, and he watched her eyebrows raise in that intriguing little quirk of hers.

"The piling's been the same for as long as I can remember, though I recall my father replacing some of the boards after a storm once or twice." She stomped her foot twice. "I believe it's very solid."

He nodded, and she turned to lead the way up to the house. The dock ended at a small rock ledge cut into the side of the hill. From there, broad, shallow steps had been carved into the granite foundation of the island in a zigzag, forming an *S* to the top of the bluff.

All along the path the shrubs and trees grew thick

and plentiful, and he imagined that in the warmer months the underbrush would be lush and lavish as well. The deciduous trees stood tall and ancient and bare of life at the moment, but they, too, added only splendor to the possibilities he was envisioning.

A low rock wall circled the cliff that looked down on the cove sheltering the boat house and dock from harsh weather. Between it and the flagstone patio in front of the house was an entire field of neatly clipped grass and carefully tended flower gardens.

"I accept your apology," he said, looking around with an appraising eye.

"For what?" she asked, startled.

"For not asking me here in the summer or fall, when this place must be spectacular."

She smiled, again affected by his praise.

"We call it the Bride's Garden because the women of my family have always tended it, and until my mother, of course, all the women came here as brides."

"No male heir, huh?" he said, walking across the lawn toward the house.

"Well, yes, there was a son before my grandfather died. But my mother's brother was killed in Germany during World War II, and my grandmother, a Jovette by marriage herself, had no one else to leave it to but my mother."

"Then she married a Wheaton, and the island eventually came to you."

"Right."

"And up until you, it's always belonged to a Jovette?"

"Since the early sixteen hundreds, yes."

He stopped cold. "That's over three hundred years."

She turned grave eyes on him. "I know that, Mr. Dunsmore."

Attempting to hang on to a legacy that was three hundred years old would undoubtedly be an awesome responsibility—certainly one he found difficult to imagine, his own family being a mishmash of steprelatives and in-laws. There was a tightening in his chest, and he encountered a wave of sympathy for her before he pushed it aside and reminded himself that her indebtedness was none of his doing.

"You know," he said slowly, his expression wary. "I'd be reluctant to mention this, except that I'm sure it's already occurred to you, but with everything else you've done to interfere with the sale of this island, why didn't you try to get it declared an historical landmark?"

She shook her head and started across the stone terrace to the front door. "I'd have to open it to the public, and then it might as well be a resort." She spoke as if resort were another name for Den of Iniquity. "It's a home, Mr. Dunsmore. Not a tourist trap."

He could have let her comments pass, he had a vague understanding of her feelings for the place, but . . .

"I don't know," he said, stepping into the house behind her and taking a slow appreciative survey of the spacious foyer, the graceful curve of the staircase to the second floor, the highly polished antiques. "I don't seem to be having any trouble seeing this as a small, intimate lobby. . . . maybe a quiet little bar in this room over here and . . . How big is the dining room, Ms. Wheaton?"

Bristling, she turned to him. Amber sparks of anger flashed in her eyes and did strange things to the rhythm of his heart. Reflex snapped her head up straighter on her neck and proud indignation stretched out her spine to a new height. It was a stance that inspired admiration.

"I wouldn't count my hotels until the neon sign goes up, Mr. Dunsmore," she said, hoping the fear and dread she was feeling wasn't evident in her voice. "I have every intention of persuading you to leave Jovette Island unmolested."

"Unmolested, Ms. Wheaton? Have you thought that I might be the one to save this place from ruin?"

"Does it look ruined to you, Mr. Dunsmore?"

"Not yet. But if you can't pay the taxes and you're behind on the mortgage payments, how do you plan to keep up the maintenance?"

"I've told you before," she said, shifting her weight uncomfortably, loath to discuss her finances with a stranger. "I can pay the taxes, catch up on the mortgage payments, and maintain this place, but I need time. Just a little time."

"Planning to win the lottery?"

"Where the money comes from isn't your concern. All I want from you is an open mind while you hear me out and your promise to stall the sale of the island for the next two or three months."

He took in a deep breath and contemplated her with many misgivings. Damn, what if she was planning to rob a bank for the money she needed? She'd end up in prison again. Somehow the idea disturbed him deeply.

"Okay. Give it your best shot," he said, sober and to his own amazement, sincere. "Convince me that I don't want this place."

With dogged steps he followed her up the stairs, resigned to the next couple of hours of whining and complaining. The roof would leak like a sieve, the support beams would have wood rot, and she'd be sure to mention the wall mice that scurried about at night. It was going to be a long afternoon.

"All the wainscoting is original, of course. My father was one of those men who couldn't sit still and relax for more than ten minutes, so he'd come here and fiddle," she said, topping the stairs. "He hung the wallpaper in the foyer and in this hallway about four years ago. I think he must have redecorated every room in this house at least twice since he and my mother married."

"And in keeping with his standing as an amateur historian, he's kept his renovations as authentic as possible," he concluded, running his hand over the pink-and-silver-striped paper above the dark polished wainscoting.

She smiled, pleased with his astuteness. He was very discerning about many things, she noticed. Would he be as intuitive and insightful as a lover? she wondered absently.

A lover? But her scheme wasn't designed to go that far. . . .

He followed her around the curve of the banister that looked down into the foyer.

"This was my parents' room," she said, opening a door at the end of a large semicircle.

That's when it started. She led him from room to room meticulously pointing out amenities, throwing dustcovers off priceless antiques, itemizing verifiable details of the house that had been maintained in perfect working order, where modern conveniences had been installed and why.

"My great-grandfather had very poor eyesight, and no matter how high they turned the gaslights, he'd keep bumping into things and tripping," she informed him. "We never did have a cable run out from the mainland, so there's no telephone.

But there is a small generator for the electricity. It was replaced about ten years ago, I guess. I'd have to check for sure, but it still runs like a top. Starts right up, every spring."

The second floor consisted of a small sitting room connected to the master suite—" . . . my mother's mother suffered with bouts of 'melancholia'—though I suspect it was more in line with PMS as she wasn't ever committed or anything, and it is a rather nice term for it, don't you think? Anyway, she spent hours at that window, staring out at the river, and my mother would have to come here to see her . . ."—and bathrooms—" . . . Benny Goodman slipped on some wet tiles in here once, threw his back out, and had to spend the rest of his visit in bed. . . ."—and a variety of bedrooms—" . . . when the Roosevelts came for the weekend, they always asked for this room. He liked to keep an eye on our neighbors to the north."

"And which is your room?" he asked with an immoderate and irrational curiosity he couldn't begin to explain, even to himself.

"There," she said with a nod. "On the end." Following him, she added, "Before it was mine, it was my mother's. Before that it was her father's. And before him, his father's."

He opened the door to a large southeast room with a huge bay windowseat. Unlike some of the other rooms with their heavy, dark Victorian colors, Harriet's room was done in light, airy colors with a profusion of lacy ruffles and thick soft pillows. It was also the only room he'd seen so far that looked lived-in. There were open books and papers on the desk, while dolls, fans, floppy hats, pictures, and other personal articles were set about. And there was a distinct feminine fragrance, unlike the scent of dust and old wax that permeated the other rooms.

A few brazen steps took him into the room where he scanned book titles and photographs, picked up a music box, examined it, and set it back down, then ran a hand along the elegant white ruffle of the canopy over her bed.

"You don't seem the frilly type," he said casually.

A smile tugged at her lips. She glanced about, seeing the familiar surroundings through his eyes, and then chuckled.

"I'm afraid I was a grave disappointment as a girl, for both my parents," she said with only pleasure in her voice. "My mother always hoped I'd carry on the Jovette tradition of being a social butterfly, but I took after the Wheatons and was introverted and bookish. And my dad always saw me as a sweet, shrinking, prissy little indoor thing instead of a nature girl who liked to fish and sail and get filthy in the gardens."

"And their disappointment amuses you," he concluded, fascinated by the faraway look in her eyes and the lopsided smile on her lips.

"No. Of course not," she said, startled. She stood by the door, waiting to close it, hoping that his inspection of her private space was over. "It wasn't like that. It was never a point of contention between us. All they truly ever wanted for me was to be happy and to be . . . whoever I was meant to be."

"And who were you meant to be, Harriet Wheaton?" he asked, walking toward her, stopping directly in front of her, standing close enough for her to see flecks of gold in his green eyes and to fill her head with the spicy scent of his after-shave.

He watched her eyes grow large and unblinking as she stared at him. She swallowed nervously, and he felt a rush of excitement. His gaze lowered to her barely parted lips, then to the erratic jumping of the pulse point at the base of her neck, then back to her mouth. His muscles tensed. An unexpected anticipation of pleasure rattled his bones.

She gave a slight shrug. Her throat felt dry and tight when she uttered, "I guess I was meant to be Harriet Wheaton."

"And who is Harriet Wheaton?" he asked. Could she possibly taste as sweet as she looked? he added silently.

Her brows rose, and she shrugged again in a fashion that was clearly her own.

"I don't think you'd believe me if I told you, Mr. Dunsmore. It's better if you find out for yourself."

Was that a dare he saw in her eyes? A challenge? The notion came and went so fast, he couldn't say for sure.

"Okay," he said, wanting to believe that he'd seen the gauntlet go down. "But I should warn you, I'm extremely thorough in all my ventures. It's one of my few virtues."

She grinned at him, unconcerned.

"What?" he asked, his eyes narrowing in suspicion when he saw her teeth clamp down on her bottom lip to keep her thoughts from escaping.

"It's nothing really," she said, attempting to close the door, forcing him onto the walkway above the foyer. "It's just that I had a feeling that if I kept at it long enough, I'd discover that you had at least one virtue."

"Very cute," he said, finding it impossible not to return her teasing grin. "But hardly the best way to win my support."

"Am I convincing you then?" Her expression was hopeful—and singularly appealing.

He took a deep breath. She smelled like wind and sunshine.

"Let's finish the tour," he said. He could see that she hadn't taken his answer as a flat-out no, which was what it should have been, he thought, not wanting to lead her on and for some tangled reason, not wanting to be too blunt or too brutal with her either.

But she wasn't convincing him not to take over her island. On the contrary, she was making it look like a better deal than he'd hoped for.

They were making their way back along the wide walkway to the center of the semicircle of doors when a childhood memory dropped from out of nowhere and hit him hard in the chest, like a anvil.

There were halls in the house he'd grown up in. Long empty halls like the one he was in now. And doors. Locked doors. He blinked, and he was a small boy, awakening from a nightmare, crying and frightened. He slips from his bed, afraid of the dark, more afraid of being alone. His bedroom door opens to more darkness, deeper and darker than what is behind him. The hallway is cold. He knows that if he were quieter, if he never made any noise at all, that his mother's room would be closer to his, instead of down the hall. He walks softly. He's not a very good boy. Mommy will be upset if he wakes her up. But if he's alone, the scary things in his room will get him. It's a very long hall, a forever hall—and there might be something following him. He walks faster. His heart races. Mommy's door! . . . is locked. He turns to face the darkness. He blinks again.

A shuddering breath escaped him. Where the hell had that come from? he wondered, shaken, cramming his memories back into a crusty old box and mentally sitting on the lid.

Harriet was ahead of him. His eyes darted about, settling on the door to her parents' room and shifting back to the door of her room at the opposite end of the semicircle. He felt a tightness in his chest and an irresistible compulsion in his heart.

"Harriet?"

"Yes?" She stopped to look at him. He'd used her given name. The tone of his voice lowered as it rumbled over the r's. She liked it.

"Were you a noisy kid?"

"Ah . . . no. I was quiet and a little shy," she said, and then for no good reason she knew, added, "I didn't make friends easily. I spent a lot of time alone, or with my parents. Why?"

The tightness in his chest increased and his heart sank.

"I thought maybe that was why your room was so far from your parents'," he said, feeling self-conscious and hot in the face.

"Oh, for pity's sake," she said with a laugh, ignorant to his discomfort. "I forgot to show you. It's one of the best things about the house, certainly one of the most fun." She stepped around him and walked briskly back toward her bedroom. "It was an addition to the house, but you can't really see it unless you know it's there."

"What?"

"Come on, I'll show you. You'll love it."

He shook his head. The Wheaton woman wasn't following the program at all. If he didn't know better, he would have sworn she was trying to get rid of the place instead of trying to save it from the auction block. What sort of game was she playing?

"My great-grandfather was a colicky baby," she was saying as she entered her room.

"Is this the same one who had poor eyesight and banged into things?"

"Yes, but that was much later, of course, when he was old." She stopped at what appeared to be a closet door. "Anyway, originally, the sitting room was a nursery. But it wasn't very big, and when my great-grandfather's tummy started to hurt, there wasn't much room to walk him around in. His nanny would sometimes take him to the third floor and walk him, but he was very loud and so the nanny and sometimes his mother used to walk back and forth around the walkway with him, and when they had guests, they kept everyone awake all night. Sooo, when he learned he was about to be a father again, my great-great-grandfather had this built into the house." She opened the door and stepped inside.

"They closed in this part of the open foyer all the way to the main floor. There are closets down there, but up here, it's a hall leading from the master suite to the new nursery, which is now my room. And these,"—she banged on the wall with her fist—"are so well insulated, you could shoot a rocket off in here and no one in the house would hear it, unless you left the doors open." There was a soft laugh. "Which is why I stayed in the nursery for so long."

He stopped his inspection of the paneled walls and the thick soft carpeting on the floor to look at her. "Run that by me again?"

"I was afraid of the dark, you see," she admitted, feeling unreasonably foolish. She hadn't seen any boogie-boys in the dark for quite some time, and childhood fears were nothing to be ashamed of, but still . . . "My parents would leave my door open, turn on this hall light and leave their door open, in case I got scared. That way they could hear me, I could hear them, and we didn't disturb anyone." She tossed her black braid over her shoulder and pushed her glasses closer to her face in one continuous motion. "I was afraid of the dark for a long time and when no more children came along, the nursery just stayed mine."

"What about sex?" he asked.

Sex? "I'm sorry?" she said. Sex?

"What about sex?"

"Well, what about it?" she asked, a bit frazzled. Sex was good. Sex was delightful. What else did he want to know about it?

"What did your parents do about sex, with you roaming around all night?"

Her features went blank. "I don't know," she said, reflecting on the past. "When I was young, I suppose they simply stopped whatever they were doing and let me crawl into bed with them. Later, we knocked before entering one another's room. It was the polite thing to do. Considerate. I never caught them at it, and I never really gave it much thought," she said, looking at him as if she considered *his* thoughts to be off track.

They were, of course. He shouldn't have asked her about it. He should have left it all in the past where it belonged. Still, there was a child in him somewhere that envied her the hall light and open doors.

"Clever idea, this," he said, his gaze roving about, avoiding her inquisitive stare. "Did someone name it? Like the Bride's Garden? My guess is the Wailing Hall."

"That's very good," she said, laughing, turning to leave. "But, no. It's just the hall to the nursery."

She took him to a door on the walkway that opened onto a stairwell. She stepped in and proceeded to the top. The third floor had at one time been servants' quarters and was now used for storage.

"Did you live here year round?"

"No. I grew up in Harford."

"New Hampshire? Massachusetts? Maine?"

"New York," she said, taking the servants' stairs all the way to the kitchen on the main floor. "Between Binghamton and Ithaca. My father was an apple farmer."

"Was an apple farmer?"

"Mm. He passed away a while back," she said.

He wished he could see her face. There was nothing in her voice to indicate that her father's passing had had any effect on her, but if he could have seen her face. . . .

"I'm sorry," he said.

"Thank you," she said, still without emotion. "The kitchen, as you can see, is completely modern. Oh. Did you want to see the attic?"

"Does it leak?"

"Certainly not."

"I didn't think so," he said. "I think we can skip it this time."

"There's a cellar too," she said uneasily. "It has rock walls so it sometimes gets a little damp, usually during long periods of steady rain. But it doesn't really leak."

"Harriet. Harriet." He shook his head. "You're doing it all wrong," he said, throwing his head back as if he couldn't take the agony of it any longer. "You're supposed to point out the flaws in the house and conceal the assets. You're talking this place up like a commission-hungry realtor."

"But . . . there are no flaws. A couple of the doors need oiling, and that faucet upstairs needs a new washer but other—"

"You'd better make up a couple more then—a couple of *big* ones—if you don't want me to snatch this place out from under you," he said, hardly believing his own ears. "Could I bother you for a drink?"

Bewildered, she nodded. "Coffee, tea, juice? Something stronger?"

"Coffee, if it's no trouble."

In a strained silence she put coffee and water in the coffee maker and then, with her hands on the counter behind her, she turned back to him.

"Would you like to see the main floor while we're waiting?" she asked, unsure of how to proceed after his outburst.

"No," he said bluntly. "I'm sure the rest of the house is as fine as what I've seen so far. I don't need to see any more." The kitchen was a bright, warm, well-used room with tall stools lined up at the center work island.

Frowning, she watched Payton straddle one of the stools and lean his elbows on the counter.

"I'm not stupid, Mr. Dunsmore." He looked at her. "If I'd brought you out here and tried to tell you the place was a shambles—when a blind man can see that it isn't—you'd have called me a liar and a cheat and refused to help me."

This was true, but he'd never intended to help her anyway.

She crossed from the sink to the island, her hands spread beseechingly.

"I've come to you in good faith, as open and honest as I can be, because I want you to see Jovette Island for what it really is—a home. My home. It isn't just another piece of real estate, it's my family's history." Her words were building up speed and momentum. "Lazare Jovette was a French trapper who traded with the Indians for this island. Gerard Jovette fought Americans to keep the island; and then, as fate would have it, by the time the boundary between Canada and the United States was decided upon, his grandson Jean had already fallen in love with and married a young American woman, and the island remained in Jovette hands. Adam Jovette fought tooth and nail to keep it when the Jovettes lost most of their money during the crash of '29 and through the depression. My own parents weren't wealthy people, they had to make sacrifices to keep this island and—" She went suddenly silent.

"And that leaves you," he said, finishing for her.

"That leaves me."

For a long moment he studied her, and when he couldn't stand seeing the sadness and the hope and touching ray of faith in her eyes any longer, he stood and resettled himself at a window. He stared out at more lawn and the dense field of trees that covered the rest of the island.

He didn't want to hurt her. He wasn't a sentimental man, and she was nothing to him but a stranger who'd caused him a great deal of aggravation. But a minute part of him, hidden deep inside, was inhibiting his usual decisive business practices, in favor of a less harsh, less cruel beat-around-the-bush method that he normally scorned.

"Are there any ghosts?" he asked, not looking at her.

"Ghosts? Of course not. Why do you ask?"

"Family homes with a history and an active ghost or two are hard to come by these days," he said, his voice dispassionate. "Antiquity is in these days. And ghosts attract tourists and thrill seekers like magnets. Though, even without the ghosts, there's enough history in this place to turn a good profit. . . . of course, we could always invent a couple of ghosts."

He'd come to her island, but he hadn't heard or seen anything except what he'd wanted to see and what he'd wanted to hear. A loud clanging noise sounded in Harriet's head. Prison bars. Her fate was sealed.

"Would a legend help?" she asked, her voice rigid with anger, her heart as hard and heavy as stone as she set her plan into action.

Three

"A legend?" he asked, turning to look at her. "What sort of legend?"

"Magic," she said. She couldn't trust the expression on her face not to betray her and busied herself pouring coffee for them both. "This island is magical."

He laughed. It was a deep, warm sound she might have enjoyed if it didn't hurt her so much.

He had to admire her. Harriet Wheaton was a woman of her word. She'd obviously seen that she hadn't convinced him not to buy the island and instead of whining and crying and begging him to reconsider, she'd accepted her failure and given up gracefully, as she'd promised. Dealing a legend into the arrangement was above and beyond what was expected of her.

"Wonderful," he said, chuckling as he took the seat across from her, where she'd placed his cup of coffee. "Magic beats a ghost hands down every time."

"It gets better," she said, guarding her features closely. "The magic involves love and living happily ever after." She paused. "I suppose that's why there are no ghosts," she added.

"This is great. A honeymooners' island!" He became solemn. "Look," he said, trying his best to be gentle—an uncommon endeavor. "I . . . I can imagine how tough this is on you and I . . . it's business. It's nothing personal. I . . . thought I was going to enjoy this part—taking your island—after all the trouble you've caused me. But . . . well, I'm not, Harriet."

He could have fooled her.

"Maybe not just honeymooners, Mr. Dunsmore," she said, ignoring his feeble excuses or apology or whatever it had been. He was extremely handsome and something very male called to the woman in her. But plainly, there wasn't a drop of human kindness or compassion in him. "You could turn it into a . . . a lonely hearts island. You know, where strangers come and meet and fall in love, and then live happily ever after."

He gave her a small smile and nodded, watching her expectantly, waiting to hear the legend. He couldn't ask her to tell him. He could hardly think, let alone speak. Something was terribly wrong. He felt no triumph, no satisfaction, no pleasure. If anything, he was feeling something that he suspected came very close to guilt. Guilt! And he'd done nothing wrong.

The facts were simple. It took money to maintain an island. She had no money. Someone was going to take the island from her eventually. It might as well be him. It made perfect sense, so what was the problem?

Was he supposed to give this strange woman the money she needed? Loan it to her, knowing she'd never be able to repay him? Walk away from an excellent investment only to have someone else snap it up behind him? Where was all this stuff coming from? he questioned, shaking his head.

"You don't believe in happily ever after?" she asked, watching his head move back and forth. He gave her a blank stare. "I sometimes wonder about it myself, but it's in the legend and I've seen proof of it."

"Of happily ever after?"

She nodded. "You remember I told you about Lazare Jovette, the French trapper who came to the island first? Well, one winter—a particularly fierce winter—he came across a young Indian girl, ill and half-frozen, right here on this very island." She paused briefly to speculate on the extent of Payton's knowledge of history. "You see, when the Europeans came to this country and Canada, they brought with them diseases that were unknown to the Indians. Whole communities were wiped out by smallpox, and even illnesses as simple as the flu took many of them because they had no tolerance built up against the white man's diseases."

"The Indian girl had smallpox," he deduced.

"No. I never heard exactly what she had, but when she became ill her people cast her out, thinking it was something terrible and wanting to save the rest of the tribe. Lazare found her, took her in, and spent the winter nursing her back to health." She took a sip of her coffee. "In the spring, her people returned. They were shocked to see that she'd survived the illness as well as the winter, and they welcomed her back. But Lazare had fallen in love with her and didn't want her to leave."

"So, he went to the chief and made him an offer he couldn't refuse," Payton injected.

"Yes. How did you know?"

"TV."

There was a twinge of resentment at his lowering Lazare's story to a TV western.

"Actually, the chief was no problem," she said. "But the girl's father loved her very much and was too happy to have her back to let her go again. He wanted her to marry a young brave and stay with the tribe. And when the girl pleaded with him and proclaimed her deep feelings for Lazare, the father still thought to discourage the union by asking an enormous price for her."

"And being a poor trapper, Jovette couldn't pay the price. So he and the girl ran off together," Payton inserted.

"Jovettes don't deal that way, Mr. Dunsmore," she informed him haughtily. "Lazare was willing to pay the price, but he didn't want the Indians to lose respect for him by making such a horrible trade. So, he told them that he'd give them a bearskin, twelve beaver hides, and seven fox pelts for the girl—and the island."

"Where are these Indians now?" he asked, grinning. "I've got a couple of bridges I could trade to them, cheap."

"I believe they've already made that deal," she said, making no attempt to hide her disapproval of his attitude.

He had the grace to sober and look sheepish. "So Jovette and the Indian girl lived happily ever after and, so the legend."

"No. That was just the beginning," she said. "They did live as happily ever after as anyone could expect to, but it didn't end there. Many years later, their son towed a drifting dory to the shores of this island and found a young Irish girl inside. She was indentured to some beastly man and was attempting an escape. She'd been on the river for several days and was weak with hunger and exhaustion, but it was love at first sight between her and Lazare's son. I think his name was Leon or maybe Antoine, I always get the two mixed up."

"So, the two of them got married and lived happily ever after and, thus the legend," Payton said, as if it were inevitable.

"Well, yes they did, but two Jovettes falling in love on the island is only a coincidence," she said. "But when it was still happening a hundred years later . . . during the French and Indian War? . . . A young English lieutenant—a bitter enemy of the French—happened upon the island and fell in love with the daughter of the house. Marie, I think. And then a few years later an American settler with two daughters, going up river in search of farming land, sought safety on the island during a summer squall, and Marie's brothers each took a wife before the settler moved on. . . . Well, *then* falling in love on Jovette Island became a bit of a legend."

"Did any Jovette ever not fall in love on the island?"

"Oh, sure. Many of them. After all, this is sort of an out-of-the-way place. It's not like there's a regular stream of traffic out here. But we've documented that at least one Jovette every generation meets, falls in love, and marries someone on the island."

"You're kidding."

She shook her head.

"Your parents met here?"

"My uncle and my father were school chums, and one summer, my uncle invited my father to spend a week here. He met my mother. They fell in love. And a few years later they married."

"You're kidding."

She shook her head again.

"What an incredible set of coincidences," he said, marveling.

"Coincidence or magic?" she asked.

He stared at her openmouthed for an instant and then laughed.

"You don't really believe it's magic, do you?"

She gave him her Harriet shrug and a Harriet lift of her brows. "Why not?"

"Because not ten minutes ago you told me you weren't stupid."

"That has nothing to do with believing in magic." She stood to put her cup in the sink. "But the magic has everything to do with keeping the island in the Jovette family."

"And why is that?" he asked, a disbelieving smirk on his lips.

"Because the magic works only for the Jovettes."

"What does that mean?"

"It means, that the Jovettes who have fallen in love here have had good marriages and lived fairly happily ever after. Whereas the Jovettes who haven't fallen in love here have generally had bad marriages that ended in divorce. And it means that, as far as we know, no one outside the family has ever met someone on the island and fallen in love with them. It means the magic works only for the Jovettes."

"That's ridiculous," he said, and then as it occurred to him, added, "This isn't another one of your tricks to keep me from buying the island, is it?"

"No, Mr. Dunsmore," she said, resigned to the fact that she was going to have to convert him the hard way. "It's another attempt at making you see that the island should remain in the Jovette family."

"Well, I'm sorry, Ms. Wheaton. But I'm not buying it. The story, that is. The island is too good a deal to pass up."

"And nothing I say will change your mind."

Honesty is always the best policy, he told himself, a part of him wishing he'd never gotten involved in the first place. *Get tough with her. Tell her about the real world. Don't let those sad brown eyes get to you.*

"I'm afraid not," he said, making a helpless gesture with his hands. "I understand what you're going through, but financially—"

"No, Mr. Dunsmore," she said, interrupting the speech she'd already heard several times before, tears welling in her eyes. "I don't think you do understand what I'm going through. You couldn't possibly." She blinked the tears away. "Would you excuse me for a few minutes, please?"

"Of course," he said, feeling that weird remorseful feeling again and hating it. He was grateful for the control that kept her from crying in front of him, indebted even.

"Help yourself to more coffee," she said over her shoulder, pushing her way through a swinging door and into the front foyer, where she ceremoniously removed her glasses, set them on the hall table, and prepared herself to do battle.

She grabbed up her slicker and exited through the door, without looking back and without a second thought until she reached the dock. She stared down at the skiff as it bobbed and lobbed against the rubber bumpers on the dock, and went over her plan one last time.

The worst possible consequence would be that she'd end up back in prison. But having lost everything that ever meant anything to her, would that be such a catastrophe? And if her plan worked, *if it worked,* she'd still have Jovette Island and a chance at a future.

Of course, that would mean that she had forced Payton Dunsmore to fall in love with her, and that wasn't really fair to him, but if he wouldn't listen to reason . . . well, what choice did she have?

She took a deep breath and blew it out through pursed lips to calm herself. It didn't help.

She stepped down into the dinghy and reached for the small black bag she'd placed in the boat earlier. With every second of time that passed, her resolve slipped. Maybe she could talk to him a little more. Maybe she hadn't been clear enough for him. Maybe she could have explained better how important the island was to her. She pulled the bag open with undue force. Maybe she should have cried. She could have pleaded and begged with him. She reached inside the bag and wrapped her fingers around a handle. She could have thrown herself on his mercy. Her index finger curled around a trigger.

Was there any better way she could have handled the situation? She didn't think so.

Aiming skyward, she pulled the trigger once, then twice, and watched the large three-quarter-inch drill bit spin around at a blinding speed. She tried the deep breaths again to no avail, then took dead aim at the bottom of the dinghy.

The battery-operated drill shot slivers of wood flying until she discovered that a little muscle was required to hold the bit in one place. But after that, the holes in the bottom of the boat became smooth, round, and plentiful.

Payton paced the kitchen with his second cup of coffee cooling in his hands. He felt lower than a doormat, and it irritated him. Why the hell did he care if she was off somewhere crying? He hardly knew the woman. He didn't even like her very much. She was a pest and a bother despite the fact that she had eyes he could swim in and a mouth that fascinated him like none he'd seen before. And her life was a mess.

She'd been to jail! The woman was a criminal. She was broke. She had no job. She had a never-was chance of keeping the island without money. And was he responsible for any of her problems? Hell, no.

So, why did he feel half-sick inside? Where was that nice, cold numbness he usually carried around to keep him from feeling this way? Why did he continue to think about going to her? And what would he say if he did? What was taking her so long? he wondered, opening the door that led to the back lawns.

He stepped out onto a flagstone terrace, smaller than the one at the front of the house, and, then onto the dry, lifeless grass beyond. His imagination ran amok with visions of the splendor and beauty that would return to the island in the spring.

Gazing eastward, he took in a better view of the gazebo he'd only glimpsed from the river. It didn't take a lot of ingenuity to picture women in stylish long dresses with large brimmed hats and parasols or men with slicked-back hair and stiff white collars and . . .

Payton put his ears to the wind, like an animal sensing danger. A noise. No. Yes, there it was again. Sea gulls called out to one another, and the noise rose up to join their clamor. A buzzing noise that was distinctly mechanical.

He followed the intermittent sounds to the front of the house, across the great lawns, toward the cove that sheltered the boat house and dock. He stood beside the low rock wall at the top of the bluff. His eyes narrowed in disbelief. A low rumble of expletives escaped him.

"Are you crazy?" he bellowed down at the female lunatic drilling holes in the bottom of the only visible means of transportation off the island. He started down the chiseled steps, muttering, "Just my luck. Stranded on an island with a crazy woman. Oh, jeez. . . . I should have checked to see what she went to prison for. . . . All that history and stuff about magic and not one word about insanity. . . . I should have guessed it when she started with all that talk about magic. . . ."

Engrossed in her holes, Harriet didn't hear or see him until he was nearly upon her. Unfortunately, even with close to two dozen punctures, the water level inside the boat barely covered the tops of her deck shoes. The boat wasn't sinking fast enough.

Quickly, as if she'd foreseen this slight problem, she cast off from the dock, *slowly* sinking several feet away.

By the time Payton reached her, he was speechless. With his suit jacket open and flapping in the wind, his fists on his hips, he gaped at her.

"I'm really sorry it has to be this way, Mr. Dunsmore," she called, lifting her voice over the wind, water, and wailing birds. "But you didn't leave me any choice. I suppose you're a bit put out with me."

She was either a wiz at understatement or her understanding of the English language was extraordinarily limited.

"Well, I can't blame you for that," she went on, trying to smile reassuringly. "I'd feel the same way. But there's a reason for this and . . . if you'll just give me a chance to explain . . . well, you'll probably still be angry, but I think you'll at least understand why I'm doing this."

"I wouldn't count on it, Ms. Wheaton," he said through clenched teeth. "And you'd damn well better have another boat hidden around here somewhere, because I'm not a man you'd want to play games with."

She had half a hull of water and her feet and ankles were numb with cold. It was only a matter of time now before the little boat sank completely. Still, treading water till she froze to death seemed a much more pleasant experience than what awaited her on the docks.

"We don't have to call this a game, Mr. Dunsmore," she said optimistically. "We could call it an experiment."

"It doesn't matter what we call it, the police are going to call it kidnapping or hijacking or . . . or maybe hostage taking."

"Oh, I'm sure they'll call it something," she said. "But I don't think they can technically call it any of those things since I'm not asking for a ransom or making any demands. In fact," she began to steel herself for the plunge, "if I were a good liar, I could probably get away with this. You know, say it was all your idea and that you did this." Her bottom was getting wet. "But I'm not a good liar, so I'll confess the whole thing to the police when it's over. If you want me to."

"When what's over?" he asked, as she jumped into the water, swimming to the ladder at the end of the dock. "When what's over?" he asked again, watching her pull herself up the ladder and step, shivering, onto the dock. Her slicker hung wet and loose from her body but the sweater and jeans beneath it were waterlogged and clinging to her slim figure. "When what's over?"

"The experiment," she said, teeth chattering, her charmingly lopsided lips blue tinged.

"What experiment?"

"Your s-skepticism about the magic . . ."

"It's more than skepticism."

" . . . is unders-standable. And I'll be hon-onest with you, M-Mr. Dunsmore, I'm not so sure it's real either." She shivered and threw her wet braid back over her shoulder. "I . . . I mean, I'm a scientist and m-magic just doesn't fit into my way of thinking. But the overwhelming frequency of Jovettes falling in l-love on this island can't be denied either."

Oh, gawd! She was blithering. Payton wanted to cry.

"I don't understand," he said.

"Well, aside from the f-fact that I love the island, the magic is another re-reason for me not to lose it."

"Lose what?"

"The island," she snapped. She was too cold for him to be acting dense all of a sudden. "What if falling in love on this island is my only chance at happily ever a-after? I'm th-thirty years old. I'm the last Jovette, the only Jovette of this generation. I-if the legend is valid and the magic exists, I can't sell the island until after I fall in love. And then what about my children?"

"What about them?" Oh, Lord! Why had he asked?

"Well, they'd be J-Jovettes by blood. They'd deserve their chance at love too."

"What does any of this love stuff have to do with me?" Dumb question—he was buying her island. "I'll tell you what, Harriet," he said, trying to sound sane and reasonable. "I'll throw an open reservation into the deal. You can come and stay anytime you like."

"We-we—" She shivered convulsively. "Well, I had a different deal in mind."

"Fine. Whatever you want. You name the terms." He glanced around. "Where's the other boat?"

"Back at the marina." Strangely enough, he looked confused. "I . . . I misled you about *Enchantment*. I said that I knew I'd live to regret selling it, which is why I haven't yet. I do still own her, but I couldn't drill ho-holes in her hull. I'll miss the skiff, but it's all f-for a good cause . . . I hope," she added under her shuddering breath.

"Look, Ms. Wheaton," he said, shifting his weight into a stance of male superiority. "I don't like games. I don't like tricks or surprises or practical jokes. I hate being manipulated. I won't tolerate a manipulating woman, any more than I'd tolerate a whiny woman or a woman who has no self-control. I demand that you tell me what you're up to and how you plan to get us off this damned island. Right now."

He seemed to have puffed up several degrees during his tirade, and she was acutely aware of his size in relation to her own small, shivering female form. The fury in his eyes stabbed at her like pointed icicles.

"Would it be safe to say that you don't like me?" she asked.

He opened and closed his mouth twice before any words came out. "That would be a safe assumption, yes."

She shivered. "Then here's the deal," she said. "There's a boat coming for us on Sunday, in seven days. If you don't fall in love with me before that time, I'll sign the island, the house, and everything in it o-over to you and s-surrender myself to the police."

"What?"

"If you can't fall in love with me during the next s-seven days on this island, it'll mean there is no m-magic, and I'll have done all of this for nothing. B-but if you can manage to overcome your anger and f-form a fondness for me . . . well, that would be some sort of proof, wouldn't it?"

"It'd prove that I'm crazier than you are," he said, an incredulous expression on his face. Then he got angry again. "I suppose you think that I'll fall in love with you and let you keep your island."

"Oh, no," she said emphatically. "I wa-want to be fair about this. I won't forget that I forced you to fall in l-love with me, if you do. And I promise I won't hold you to it. Come Sunday all ties are s-severed. You go back to your life and I turn myself over to the police so you can press ch-charges, and I'll confess to anything you want me to. A-And as for the island, well, we'll have proof of its magic by then, one way or another, and I'll leave its destiny to your conscience."

"Are you crazy?" he asked again, sure that she must be, though she didn't look it. She looked calm and rational, as if she knew what she was doing. "If I don't check back with my office tonight, as I always do, my staff is going to have every law enforcement agency in this state out looking for me."

"Maybe not," she said, stepping around him, heading for a hot bath.

"What does that mean? Maybe not. What have you done?" he asked, following her.

"The fax I asked the desk clerk to send for me before we left the inn was to your office, informing them of your change in plans, that you'd decided to spend the holiday with friends; that you weren't to be disturbed and that you'd contact them next Monday."

"Where the hell do you get off—my staff won't buy that, you know," he said, almost gleeful that his solitary lifestyle was going to foil her plan.

"Why not?"

He had so few personal attachments, that he usually spent his holidays alone—but he didn't want her to know that. "Because . . . because I lead an an organized and orderly life. I never go off for days at a time without making arrangements ahead of time."

"In other words, your life lacks spontaneity." She looked back over her shoulder at him and smiled.

He repaid her with a grimace. "For your information, Ms. Wheaton, my life lacks nothing. I do what I want, when I want, for whatever reason I choose."

"That *is* pretty much the same st-story I got," she said, topping the stairs, heading for the house at a brisk pace. He had to jog-walk to keep up with her. "Which is why I assumed that no one would be s-surprised if you suddenly changed your plans."

"What do you mean, that's the story you got?"

She stopped short and he tripped over her.

"Well, you don't think I'd st-strand myself on an island with someone I knew nothing about, do you?"

"I have no idea what you're capable of."

"I had you investigated."

"You had me . . . ?" He realized he was talking to the wind. He sprinted to her side. "You had me investigated? By whom?"

"A v-very nice man by the name of Larry DeLuca of DeLuca Detective Agency in Tampa. He's a cousin to the detective who was recommended to m-me by a friend in New York who recently got divorced."

"Who?"

"Who is my recently divorced friend? Or who is the detective she recommended, who had a cousin in Tampa?"

"Who's this DeLuca character?" he asked, revealing his frustration as his voice rose several octaves higher. "I have people checked out all the time, and I never heard of a DeLuca Detective Agency in Tampa."

"I never actually met the man, we talked over the ph-phone." Her dockers made loud squishing noises as she crossed the terrace to the door. "And I would suspect there's a great many th-things going on in Tampa that you don't know about, Mr. Dunsmore. It is a rather large city, isn't it?"

"Did he have references? I bet you didn't even get references from this guy," he said, trailing her wet footprints into the house. "How do you know he wasn't a scam artist who fed you a lot of bogus information on me? How do you know I'm not a serial killer or a rapist or . . . or a satanist who thrives on human sacrifice? I could be a—"

"Are you?" she asked pointedly, turning on the stairs to face him.

"Are . . . No!" he said, screwing up his handsome face, too taken back to think of a good lie, one that would scare her into changing her plans. Quite extraneously, he noticed that she wasn't wearing her glasses and that her eyes were clear and bright; dark and mysterious at the same time.

"Then Mr. DeLuca didn't ch-cheat me." She resumed her ascent, her teeth chattering like castanets.

"So, I'm not a maniac—most people aren't. How do you know anything else he told you about me is true? My routine, my habits, my—ha! my appointments. I have appointments and meetings scheduled all this week. Someone's bound to notice when I don't show up."

"You canceled everything for the rest of the week in your fax, remember?" She paused. "Or did I forget to tell you? It'll all be rescheduled for next week."

"How dare you?" he shouted, outraged. "Who the hell do you think you are, marching in and mucking up my life like this? What gives you the idea—"

"You're absolutely right, Mr. Dunsmore," she said, stopping with her foot on the next step and turning to face him. Lord, she had the longest, thickest eyelashes he'd ever seen. "What I've done is unspspeakable, and I want you to know that I'm sincerely sorry." The big, dark eyes were so compelling, he almost believed her. "I wish you could see this from

my s-side, though. This is . . . this is like my last
stand, my final round, my . . . my last chance to
salvage the rest of my l-life. Don't you think that
I thought long and hard about this before I decided to do it? Don't you th-think I would have much
preferred to convince you with words rather than
action? Don't you th-think I wish you were a reasonable, compassionate man? Don't you th-think
that I know what'll happen to me if this doesn't
work? If you still hate me on Sunday, I'm g-going
to prison for the rest of my life." She held her hands
out to him, seeking his understanding. "But that's
what I'm doing, Mr. Dunsmore. I'm risking the rest
of my l-life on the hope that there's a touch of magic
on this island for me . . . and a spark of humanity
in you. Because without one my life will have no
purpose or meaning, and without the other it will
have no value."

Payton knew he could be a little self-centered sometimes—all right, so he'd cut himself off from the rest
of the world and stayed pretty much self-absorbed
most of the time—but he could still remember fear
and anguish when he saw it. They'd been friends of
his once, before he'd allowed the cold numbness to
settle in and take over his life.

"Look, I'm sure you think that you have good reasons for what you're doing. But it doesn't matter how
righteous your motivation is, holding me hostage is
wrong," he said calmly.

"I know that," she said, annoyed with his pon-
tificating. "And I wouldn't have d-done it if you'd
showed the slightest willingness to understand my
position. But you wouldn't. You c-came here with
your mind made up, and you weren't listening to
me. Well, I've got your attention n-now, don't I, Mr.
Dunsmore?"

"All right," he said, recognizing the truth of her words. "I admit that I wanted this island, and that nothing you said would have changed my mind. But I'm not as unreasonable as you think. I do understand your feelings about this place and . . . and maybe we can work something out."

"Like what?"

"Well, I don't know yet," he said, but he knew her eyes were more radiant, dazzling really, when they weren't protected by her glasses—almost the way diamonds sparkled brighter when removed from a jeweler's display case.

He was off track. What had he been saying? Oh, yes. "But we could go back to St. Peter's Bay and discuss it. You have my solemn vow that I won't take any action until we've come to an amicable arrangement. One we can both live with."

It was Harriet's turn to question his mental stability.

"I'm supposed to b-believe that? Your solemn vow?" she asked. She'd once pledged her devotion to the King of Endless Promises, and too late discovered him forgetful.

"I am a man of my word, Ms. Wheaton," he said. Granted, he'd been called a cold, hollow shell of a human being—but no one had ever labeled him a liar before. He was nothing if not honest, because there wasn't anything he wanted bad enough to lie for and there was nothing he was afraid of losing by telling the truth.

"Prove it," she said. "Stay here and think up your amicable arrangement. And w-while you do that, I'm going up to take a hot bath. Excuse me."

"Harriet, don't do this," he called after her. "It'll only get you into more trouble. Listen to me. I promise I'll—"

Her bedroom door slammed back the rest of his words. Temporarily defeated, he lowered himself to sit on the steps. "I th-think I'm in d-deep t-trouble," he muttered.

Four

Heaven was a hot bath with lilac-scented bubbles. The thought floated through Harriet's mind on a hazy pink cloud, her body temperature somewhere between bone-shattering cold and warm goo. Her eyes were closed; her mouth was open, lips lax. She couldn't tell if she was still breathing, and she didn't really care.

She smiled and slid down until she felt bubbles bursting under her chin. Did real criminals learn as much in prison as people who weren't really criminals? she mused, thinking it a shame that it had taken her eighteen months of showers to give hot bubble baths their due. Bubble baths and open spaces without fences and quiet and sugary breakfast cereal and more than two pairs of shoes to choose from and the wind in her face and . . .

Her eyes popped open, and she slowly turned her head toward the door that separated her bedroom from the bath. There was silence, and then the noise came again. Whistling, soft and low. Someone was in her bedroom.

"Mr. Dunsmore?" she called, holding her breath.

"Yes?"

"You're in my bedroom."

"Yes."

"What are you doing?"

"Snooping through your drawers."

She frowned. "I'm glad to hear that you're making yourself at home, but my room is off-limits, Mr. Dunsmore."

"So was my life, Ms. Wheaton, until you decided to kidnap me."

"I didn't kidnap you. I—"

"Yeah, yeah. No ransom. No demands. Face it, kidnapping is kidnapping."

"I'm as stranded here as you are until Sunday. Couldn't we just say that I stranded us here?"

"If that would make you feel better."

"Oh, yes. Much better."

"Then no. We'll stick with kidnapping," he said, abandoning his efforts to search her room quietly, slamming a drawer shut. "Which reminds me, what happens if something . . . happens? Say, one of us gets hurt. Like you, for instance. Is there any way to get help out here?"

"Is that a threat or are you trying to scare me, Mr. Dunsmore?" Her bath was turning tepid, and she shivered. She was losing her bubbles, too, she noted absently. "Or is it a test to see how serious I am about this and how well I planned for it? Or are you really worried about my safety and well-being?"

"Oh please, Ms. Wheaton, I'm deeply concerned about your safety and well-being, of course."

"Of course," she said, smiling at the don't-make-me-laugh tone of his voice. She liked his quick, sarcastic humor. It meant he was intelligent and world wise, shrewd and clever. "Well, as it happens, Mr. Dunsmore, I did plan for such incidentals as illness and injuries. And should anything happen to me, I'll save my last dying breath to tell you how to get yourself rescued. Does that make you feel any better?"

"Absolutely," he said, only half-attentive. There was a picture of her parents on her dresser. She might be thoughtful and quiet like her father, but she looked like her mother. The same dark hair and big dark eyes; the charmingly crooked smile. They shared the trim, healthy, robust look and . . . there was a warmth and openness in their expressions that was uncanny.

"Uh-oh. You're being awfully quiet out there," she said. "Have you found something that interests you?"

"I'll say. I had you pegged for a sturdy cotton girl, and here's all these skimpy silk and lace underthings. My-oh-my, Ms. Wheaton. You're just one surprise after another." A brief pause. "If you've got a towel handy, use it."

"For what?"

"Anything you want, but I'm coming in," he said. And then he did.

"Do you mind?" she asked, sinking lower in the tub and pushing bubbles in the most judicious directions. She glowered at him.

"Of course not," he said. "Carry on."

He opened her medicine cabinet and studied the contents; found nothing that grabbed his interest and moved on to her cosmetics. The whole inspection wouldn't have taken two seconds, but his eyes kept wandering to the big claw-foot bathtub and the flushed, rosy naked woman who lay just below bubble level.

"Really, Mr. Dunsmore, couldn't you have waited until I finished my bath? I don't mind your prowling around, but my water's getting cold. Couldn't this wait—"

"I've been thinking," he said, perching himself on the lid of the commode, crossing his legs, leaning back against the tank, and twisting his arms across his chest to watch her bathe. "If we're going to experience magic together, shouldn't we call each other by our first names? Call me old-fashioned, but an impassioned woman screaming out, 'Please, Mr. Dunsmore. Now, Mr. Dunsmore,' is a little too formal for my tastes. I prefer casual sex and to be on a first name basis with my partners." He wrinkled his nose at her. "It's friendlier that way."

"Friendlier?" she asked. She swallowed hard. Was it her imagination, or was her bath water heating up again? "I . . . I . . ."

"You have been tested, haven't you?"

"Tested?"

"Harriet," he said, giving her an artful smile, enjoying the sudden panic in her expression. "You're not going to play coy with me, are you? You had me going for a few minutes, but now we both know why you lured me here and sank the boat. And I don't mind telling you, I'm flattered. Would you like me to wash your back?"

"What?" Oh, Lord! He thought . . . "Mr. Dunsmore—"

"Payton."

"Mr. Dunsmore, you've—"

"Payton."

"Payton, you've got this all wrong. It's not like that."

"It's not like what?"

"I did lure you out here, but not for sex."

"You did think to bring condoms, I hope. If you haven't actually had the blood test done, then maybe we should be cautious until we can get you checked out," he said, nodding sagely.

"I've been checked, and we won't need any condoms," she said, more than a bit flustered. Her cheeks felt on fire. She was so hot, she expected the bath water to start putting off steam.

"Great," he said, grinning, his gaze lowering to her blanket of bubbles. "Want me to do your back now?"

"No. I want you to go."

"Can't," he said with a shrug.

"Why not?"

"No boat." Razzing her was irresistible. Lord, she was cute in a dither. She'd piled her thick black braid on top of her head, making her neck look longer and so inviting.

"I meant, go from this room. Get out. Now."

"Harriet. You don't have to hide yourself from me. I've always found female bodies to be quite beautiful. You have nothing to be ashamed of."

"I'm not ashamed," she said in her defense. "I want—"

"Good," he said, cutting her off. "I was worried. I like sex with the lights on. Then all the senses are stimulated." He listed them slowly, "Sight. Sound. Touch. Taste. Smell. It's much better that way, don't you think?"

"Will you please leave? I'd like to get out now." She used her best stern schoolteacher voice this time—not that it made much of an impression on him.

"Fine. I'll dry you off, if you like."

"Like hell. Get out this minute, or I'll . . ." She stopped to watch a slow smirk spread across his lips.

"Please, continue. You'll what?"

She glared at him. It didn't frighten him.

They remained just so, him smirking, her scowling for long seconds, measuring, gauging, evaluating each other.

He couldn't stop himself. He got to his feet like a man with a purpose, turned as if to leave, then reached out and snagged her towel from the rack. He unfolded it and watched as her eyes widened and her brows lifted. He shook it out and with both arms extended invitingly, he stepped to the side of the bathtub.

"Mr. Dunsmore . . ." She wanted to sound angry and indignant. Her voice squeaked like a mouse's.

"Payton."

"Payton. . . ." Her heart was beating in her throat, choking her.

"What happened to your glasses?" he asked absently, half-mesmerized.

"My . . . they're downstairs."

"Don't you need them?"

"Not to take a bath," she muttered, caught up in his fixation. "I'm nearsighted."

Abruptly he was all business again. He dropped one end of the towel and handed her the other. "Dry off and get dressed. I'm dying to hear about your prison experience."

"My prison experience?" she said, startled, but then he was gone.

She sighed, her forehead wrinkled with worry. She hadn't really speculated on what might happen once she sank the boat, simply assuming, she supposed now, that the island's magic would take it from there and they would either fall in love or they wouldn't. She hadn't expected to feel awkward and nervous. She'd planned to be in complete control.

It was a miscalculation. A big one. She hadn't factored in the possibility that Mr. Dunsmore would have a mind and a will and a few ideas of his own on how to proceed—now that he'd accepted the notion that he wasn't going anywhere until Sunday.

* * *

The Fates were smiling on him. The nut case had a contingency plan. There was a way to get off the damned island before Sunday. All he had to do was to convince her to use it.

The big-bad-wolf routine was fun, and it had certainly made her jumpy, but . . . well, people could get carried away on that stuff, he thought, recalling how tempted he'd been to dive into that tub of bubbles with her.

Acting out the homicidal maniac wouldn't work either. She wasn't afraid of him—she never had been. And if he were going to kill her, he'd have already done it down on the beach. The time was past for such splendid thoughts, though he couldn't help but wonder if the investigator she'd hired had given her a straight line on who he was. The last person to cause him this much trouble had been a summer tutor his mother had hired to keep him occupied during his vacation from school. He'd been sixteen and ready to teach the world—and his mother—a thing or two about Payton Dunsmore IV.

He'd made a few mistakes in the beginning, but he'd known immediately that he liked calling the shots and that he didn't like being crossed. He came to value loyalty and dedication in people, rather than words of love and devotion.

But that was neither here nor there, he decided, pushing his tall frame from a soft leather chair to fix himself another drink.

He'd showed himself through the rooms on the first floor. They were beautifully decorated, stuffed with antiques and, like the other unused rooms in the house, shrouded in dustcovers. Only Harriet's bedroom and bath, the kitchen, and the library looked lived-in.

He liked the library. Books lining all four walls, circled by a catwalk, the large room felt close and cozy and friendly. Despite the copyright dates in some of the books and the number of first edition collectibles scattered throughout the shelves there was a . . . youthfulness about the room, almost as if the words and wisdom contained within stayed endlessly young, waiting to appeal to any fresh, inquiring mind that happened by.

There were two huge mahogany desks, one positioned near each of the floor-to-ceiling windows to catch the light. The sound of his footsteps was muffled in a thick area rug, woven in warm hues of gold and russet. Soft brown leather wing chairs and ottomans were pulled close to the six-foot fireplace. It would be a homey room any season of the year, he imagined.

He rubbed the dull ache in his temples and paced. It could have been the Library of Congress and not a single volume would contain the answer to his present dilemma.

There had to be a way to get around her. Talking reason to a woman, sane or not, was a waste of breath. And Harriet was not only a woman, she was a willful and resolved woman. God help him, she was a woman with a cause, which meant she'd see her foolish scheme through to the end.

Thinking about it made his head hurt more. He needed to think clearly. The answer was most likely quite simple, if he could just get a handle on it. A rescue fire on the beach? Smoke signals? If there was a chance that someone on a passing cargo ship or ferry or tug or even a fishing boat would hear him, he could scream his lungs out for help.

"Damn the woman," he said, sitting back down in a chair by the empty fireplace. What would induce her to abandon this madness, short of disaster, injury, or illness?

The tense throbbing in his forehead started to break up and scatter. His lips curled upward at the corners. A germ of an idea took root in his mind, then bloomed in a matter of seconds. Suddenly he was feeling much better.

"Mr. Dunsmore? Payton?" Harriet said a short while later, alarmed, having entered the library to find Payton sprawled out in a chair, a leg flung over one armrest, his face buried in the bend of his shirtsleeve. "What is it? Are you all right?" She hurried to his side.

"Do I look all right?" he asked, his voice weak, barely a whisper.

"No. You don't. Are you ill? Is there something I can do for you? Are . . . are you in pain?"

"Pain. Yes. Excruciating." His arm fell away from his face in a listless fashion.

"Where? Where do you hurt, Payton?" she asked, gravely concerned.

He groaned. "Everywhere. All over. Head. Neck. Shoulders. Stomach. Legs."

"Oh, my. I'm so sorry. This is all my fault. Do you have migraines, Mr. Dunsmore-ah-Payton?" she asked, her expression empathetic. "My mother had them occasionally. They were awful. And I haven't fed you. When did you eat last?"

He had her now, he thought, inwardly chuckling. He waved his arm vaguely. "Breakfast?"

"Good, but that's still been a while. It's probably the stress and tension of all this," she said, filled with guilt. She threw her thick braid back over her shoulder. "It would give anyone a headache."

"Stomach too."

"Oh. I am so sorry." He opened his eyes and gave her a pitiful look. She wasn't wearing her glasses again, he noted. Her eyes were big and warm with compassion; her brows bent with worry and remorse. She placed a comforting hand on his cheek, cool and soothing and caring. It almost blew his performance—she was truly distressed! "Would it help to lay down, do you think? That's why I came looking for you. I had hoped all along that I wouldn't have to go through with this. I didn't even prepare a room for you. Was there, I mean, do you have a preference? There are plenty of rooms to choose from."

He moaned and closed his eyes, as if making a decision would be too painful a process for his brain.

"Should go back," he muttered. "See the hotel doctor."

"I don't have much, but I think I have something for your pain, and you can rest over here on the couch while I make up your bed," she said, as if she hadn't heard his suggestion. She eased his leg off the arm of the chair. "Do you think your stomach could tolerate a little soup or something?"

With a pathetic sigh, he allowed her to assist him to his feet. Taking small, old-man steps and leaning on her heavily—liking the strength beneath the softness of her—he shuffled over to the couch.

"There you go," she said, a bit winded with the exertion. "Lay your head down now and rest. I'll be back in a jiffy."

"Suite," he mumbled when he guessed her to be close to the doorway.

"I'm sorry?" She came back to him, bending low to catch his words.

"Master suite." It had been an impulsive choice on his part, but the more he thought about it, the better he liked it. If he couldn't drum up enough symptoms to make her think he was dying, he could always wear her down by running her cute little behind off.

"Oh, yes. The master suite. Certainly. I'll only be a minute."

His eyes rolled heavenward as he mentally counted her steps to the door. "Water?"

"I missed that," she said, coming back and bending low. She smelled like lilacs. "Can I get you something?"

He took a deep breath, filling his head with a scent of springtime. "Could I bother you for some water?"

"I was just going after some." She patted his shoulder reassuringly. "You rest now. Think happy thoughts."

Happy thoughts . . . Lilacs. Bubbles. A long black braid sprouting flyaway curls. Pale, flushed naked skin. Fathomless dark eyes a man could get lost in. . . . How come his doctor never prescribed happy thoughts?

Harriet rushed into the room moments later with a mild analgesic and a glass of water. She got to her knees and tended him with unselfish mercy.

"There," she said, placing a cool, calming hand to his brow, as if it were the most natural thing in the world for her to do. "I'll have your bed made by the time those go to work and then you can go upstairs and, hopefully, sleep the rest of the pain away. I'll have a nice supper ready when you wake up, and soon you'll be right as rain again."

His groaning grunt was a warning for her not to count on it.

"Can I get you anything before I go?"

A feeble shake of his head.

"I'll hurry."

He opened one eye to watch her go. "Cold," he said, when she reached the door.

It was a good sixteen feet from the door to the couch. She crossed them patiently, bending at the waist to hear his newest complaint.

"I'm so cold," he murmured.

"I'll get you a blanket. Can I get you anything else while I'm at it?"

"No. No. Don't want to be a bother. . . ."

"It's no bother, Mr. Duns—Payton," she said softly. "I know that what I did is stressful to you. I'm the cause of your pain."

No lie.

"Just . . . the blanket," he said, controlling his deep hardy voice to a sad little whine. "Please."

"I'll be right back."

It's written in stone, sweetheart, he thought, enjoying himself immensely. It was like payback for everything she'd done to him since the first time he'd heard her name.

He waited until she'd left the room this time and then raised his voice by a hair. " . . . ice . . . pain."

"Did you say something?" she asked, hurrying back into the room and over to the invalid.

"I . . . I just thought that perhaps some ice . . . a cool compress would lessen the pain."

"Oh, that's a good idea. I should have thought of it." She started to leave and turned back. "Can you think of anything else that might help?"

"Not at the moment, no," he uttered wearily. But he'd work on it.

He had a good solid list of demands by the time she returned, but she nursed him so gently and sympathetically that he simply couldn't bring himself to use any of them. In truth, her diligent pampering was something new to him. It made him a little uncomfortable. Not to the extent that he couldn't tolerate it, but certainly to the point where he could appreciate it—had he really been in need.

She left him warm and cool respectively, and wondering how long it would be before she called for help.

Payton's sick headache was unfortunate, but nothing some rest and food wouldn't cure, she was sure. Actually, it was a stroke of luck, she decided, tucking the sheets in at the foot of her parents' bed.

She had no idea how he'd found out about her having been in prison, but discussing her conviction and incarceration wasn't something she relished. It was behind her, and she wanted to forget it.

But no one seemed to want to let her forget. Potential employers wouldn't hire her. Old friends couldn't look her in the eye. Acquaintances stopped calling. Close companions asked about it constantly, thinking it best for her to vent her emotions, when forgetting would have been more therapeutic. Every time she turned around it was there, haunting her. It was as if she had a scarlet letter stitched on everything she wore.

And now Mr. Dunsmore—Payton—knew about it. The fact that he had the information wasn't as disturbing as the thought that the knowledge would work at cross-purposes with the magic. Who could fall in love with a convicted felon?

It was a stiff blow to her scheme, no doubt about it. He was bound to ask about it again eventually, and she was bound to tell him the truth, because it was her nature. The optimist in her was beaten and threadbare, but she wanted to believe that there was still some way for her to overcome the black mark in his eyes.

She whipped her braid back over her shoulder with a shake of her head. It wasn't her intention to spend the rest of her life defending herself against a crime she hadn't committed in the first place. If Payton Dunsmore were any other man on earth, she wouldn't even attempt an explanation. But she wanted her island. And she needed his help to keep it. Therefore, she would have to win his approval.

Between the last step into the foyer and the door of the library, she mustered a cheerful smile.

"Payton?" she called softly, thinking him asleep. He grunted. "Are you feeling any better?" A groan. "Your room is ready. Do you think you'd like to try and go upstairs? I think you'd be more comfortable there, but you can stay where you are if you'd like."

"I think I can make it," he whimpered, anxious to begin round two. "Would you . . . Could I impose on you to help me a bit?"

"Of course," she said graciously, hastening to his aid.

Lord, the man was big, and heavier than he appeared, she ruminated, staggering under his weight, saved from a good crushing when he righted himself and pulled her up closer to his body.

"I feel so weak," he professed apologetically. "I can't remember ever feeling worse."

"I'm so sorry," she said, panting, taking another stair step. "I feel awful about this."

"Not your fault," he said, an accusing undertone in his voice. "How could you have known it would affect me like this?"

"I'm sure you'll feel better soon." She was too encouraging, and he smirked, his head above hers as she stooped to her task.

It was wonderful. He'd been wanting to touch her again, and he'd created the perfect happenstance to indulge his whims. When he wanted to discover if her hair was as smooth and soft as it looked, he brushed his hand across it. He gave in to the urge to ascertain exactly how well she'd fit in his arms, if he wrapped one around her waist and the other around her shoulders. He returned several times to see if the reaction he got when he rubbed the palm of his hand against her breasts was reflex . . . or something else. But the most fun was waiting for opportunities to drop his hands to the soft, round counters of her bottom and to dally there until she could manage to brush him away. A cunning ruse. He was a genius.

"I've heard that headaches like this can last for days with some people," she was saying, gasping for air. "But my mother's never lasted for more than a few hours. She used to say it was the air here, that the fresh air sort of cleared the pain out of her head."

He humphed dubiously. Air wasn't going to cure him, unless it came in pressurized tanks, on a *boat.*

"Okay, here we go, ah, Payton. Just sit. . . ." He let her ease him down onto the edge of the bed.

"Maybe I should undress."

"What?"

"Well, don't you think I'd be more comfortable in the bed if I took off my shoes and pants?" He wanted to rub his hands together with glee, but extended one shoed foot instead. She looked from his face to his foot and back in confusion. "It hurts to bend over," he said.

"Oh." Adorably addled, she stooped to remove first one shoe then the other, stepping back when she was finished.

"My pants?" he said, amused to see her face and neck turning red. "If you could help me stand . . ."

In an agitated movement she was at his side, supporting his arm. "No, I think if you stand here in front of me, with your hands on my waist here . . ." He placed her hands on his ribs above his waist and his hands on her shoulders. "I think I can stand, but if the room starts to spin, I might fall."

"I'm here," she muttered, trying to sound reassuring. But reassuring for whom, him or herself?

With inordinate slowness and immense relish he got to his feet, standing so close to her that he could feel her warm breath through the fabric of his shirt. Her gaze was riveted to the second button.

His libido was wide awake and paying close attention to her reactions, like the trembling of her hands at his sides when his fingers brushed against her midsection, reaching for his belt buckle. He inched forward, wanting her to feel his every motion.

He stopped smiling, and he didn't feel particularly playful when she raised her eyes to his. They were warm and wondrous, wild and worried, not a reflection of his own emotions. He felt the clutching in his belly, and his muscles contracted. Something primitive in him knew that if she made the slightest movement, he'd take her to the floor. Something just as primal hoped she would do something, and he couldn't forego tempting her.

In the tight quarters between their bodies, he worked his belt buckle loose. Watching the slight parting of her lips, he heard her sharp intake of air. He quickened, instinctively responding to her arousal. The slow, soft rasp of his zipper had her swallowing convulsively—they were both as stiff and unmoving as cardboard cutouts.

The disappointment was acute when he pushed his pants past his hips and she stood, unwavering, while they slipped to the floor. Immediately, she stepped back, narrowed her field of vision to the front of his shirt, and eased him back to the bed—his shirttail barely covering him to midthigh.

"I . . . I have something for you," she said, walking so briskly through the door and down the hall to the nursery that if he'd tried to stop her, she would have sustained whiplash.

"Mr. DeLuca was very thorough," she called back through the hidden corridor. "I didn't ask how he got the information—I hope it wasn't illegal—but he assured me that it was accurate . . ." she was huffing and puffing her way back to his room " . . . so I hope all this fits you."

She wrestled a large suitcase into the room and set it in the middle of the floor. She flipped her braid over her shoulder and smiled, pleased with herself.

"A suitcase?" he asked.

"Full of clothes," she said. "In your sizes. The sizes Mr. DeLuca gave me." When he remained speechless, she waddled the heavy bag to the side of the bed and braced herself before she hoisted it up onto the bed. "There. You should find everything you need. Toothpaste and toothbrush. Comb, brush, shaving stuff. Shirts and . . . well, you look through it and get ready for bed while I go get you something to eat. Do you think your stomach will tolerate a bit of food now? You really should try to eat something." Her arms flapped at her sides. "If . . . if there's anything I forgot to get or something else you want, well, there's plenty of my father's things still here, and there's bound to be something you can make do with."

She smiled at his dazed expression and turned to leave.

In stunned silence he sprang the locks on the suitcase. The uppermost garments caught and held his attention.

"What are these?" The persnickety tone in his voice stopped her cold.

"What?"

He extracted two pairs of flannel pajamas. One of a bold Bert and Ernie design, the other set in a repeating pattern of Mickey and Minnie in startling, and somehow sacrilegious, sexual positions.

"Pajamas," she said, guileless. "I wasn't sure if you were the last man on earth who still wore them to bed or not, and it does get very cold here at night. I tried to cover all the possibilities."

He was getting an education from the mouse diagrams and didn't look up. She misunderstood his silence.

"I . . . I was angry with you when I bought those," she said.

A roar of laughter quivered at the back of his throat. For a pain in the patootie, she wasn't so bad, he thought, liking her spirit. Would any ordinary kidnapper go to such lengths to insure such amenities for his victims? Ha! He hadn't enjoyed anyone quite so well in a long, long time.

"I understand," he said, tossing her token of revenge back into the suitcase before he performed a spectacular tragedy of discomfort in the rubbing of his brow. "Fortunately, I sleep nude."

"Oh. Well." He couldn't tell if she approved of his sleeping habits or not, only that they made her nervous. "I'll get you some food."

"I'm not really hungry," he said, trying to look tormented. "What I'd really like is a—well, never mind. I've inflicted enough on you already."

"No you haven't," she said, her gaze darting to his lap and swiftly away. "I mean, well, you haven't been an imposition. Please. What is it you'd like? If I have it, it's yours."

"You're sure?"

"Yes. Of course. Please. If there's anything that'll make you more comfortable . . ." Her hands waved encouragingly.

"A massage," he said, his sigh a perfect level of wistful. "I'd give my left arm for a really good rub."

Five

A really good rub?

Harriet rejected one body oil and lotion after another, in search of one that met Payton's exact specifications. Not too oily, not too fragrant. If she didn't have unscented, something light and not too feminine would suffice. And nothing with lanolin, it had to be aloe, because lanolin irritated his skin.

Provoked beyond her endurance, she growled. Were all men such infants when they were sick? she wondered. She was no criminal, but she wasn't a saint either! She wasn't sure how many more of Mr. Dunsmore's mewling requests she could handle. Who would have thought that someone so powerfully male could be such a crybaby?

A wayward pang of conscience stopped her, reversing her thoughts.

Mr. Dunsmore wasn't so bad, she conceded, giving him the benefit of the doubt. He hadn't asked to be stranded on the island with her, and it wasn't his fault he was ill. He was bossy and demanding and full of himself, but he was still a human being—of sorts.

And what if his ailment wasn't simply a tension headache? What if it was some hideous brain disorder that needed emergency medical treatment hours ago? What if he died?

What had she been thinking? It would be prison for kidnapping him; death row if she was responsible for his death. She clasped a bottle of lotion in both hands, pressed the cool container to her forehead and closed her eyes. What had her life come to? She wasn't a good criminal. It was scary and confusing; it made her stomach hurt. What had happened to her? What had she done to herself?

Lord, what had she done to Payton Dunsmore?

It was time to give up, she decided firmly. Her scheme had been harebrained from the beginning. She shouldn't have tried it. It was time to put a red lantern in the middle third floor window. Time to be rescued. It was time to give it up and get Mr. Dunsmore the care he needed, time to give up the island, time to give up her dreams and hopes for the future, time to give up period.

"Mr. Dunsmore," she called halfway down the hidden hall to the master suite. "I have some good news for you. You can relax now. I—"

"—found some lotion," he said, finishing the sentence for her. "Great. It took you so long, I was beginning to lose hope."

He came slowly to a sitting position and flung his legs over the side of the bed. In Harriet's book, long, sinewy, naked male legs, sprinkled with coarse black body hair, below tan boxer shorts and a white dress shirt, were an extremely intimate sight. It threw her a little off course.

"I . . . I . . . I . . ."

He gave her a humble smile, pretending not to notice that she'd gone suddenly dysfunctional.

"I'm afraid I'm still a little dizzy," he said, his eyes pleading. "I'll need your help to get my shirt off."

"Off?"

He nodded. "It's best that way. Deeper penetration . . . of the muscles. And the lotion works better without the shirt."

Goodness, he was handsome. But being in the same room with him made her as jumpy as a cat with its tail on fire. She set the lotion down on the table beside the bed.

"Is there a best way to do this?" she asked, reluctant to touch him until she absolutely had to.

"Well, I think I can hold myself upright, if you could unbutton my shirt and take it off for me."

Ah, jeez. Was it her? Or was undressing a man you barely knew accepted etiquette these days? It didn't seem to bother him. Could she be any less casual about it?

He stood tall and straight at the side of the bed. His gaze was a tangible thing on her hair, her face, her trembling fingers as she concentrated on what was becoming an impossible task. When did they start making the holes and buttons on men's shirts so small? She was tempted to get a magnifying glass. She wasn't normally so clumsy, was she?

"I'm sorry this is taking so long," she muttered, her cheeks flushed and hot. Her eyes kept darting back to the sparse mat of hair on his chest. Every time a button came loose, more of the trail of hair down the middle of his stomach was revealed, with more golden skin and more rounded muscles.

"You're doing fine," he murmured, his voice soft, like a caress.

His after-shave was subtle but heady—well, it was going straight to her head anyway. It was like an invitation to bury her nose in his chest and breathe in deeply the way she would a flower.

"There," she said, triumphant, stepping away from

him. "Done. Would you . . . would you like something to wear, like pajama bottoms, sweatpants or something."

"No. Thank you." He hesitated. "Unless, of course, you're uncomfortable."

"Who me? No, no, no. As long as you're comfortable." She saw his grimace of pain as he struggled to remove his shirt. "Here, let me help." She pushed it past his shoulders and tugged it off over his hands. And there he was—towering, virile—in his underwear. She could feel her knees and elbows melting. "How . . . How should we do this? I told you I wasn't very good at it. Inexperienced, I mean."

"Relax, Harri," he said, crawling onto the bed, lowering himself to his abdomen. "Do you mind if I call you Harri?"

"Not many people do anymore." She took up the lotion and frowned at it. How much should she use? "It fit when I was a kid. But I'm more of a Harriet now, I think."

"Well, I like it, so do you mind?" He was poofing his pillow into just the right shape.

"No."

"Good. Anyway, relax. There's no wrong way to do this."

"How much should I use?"

"Some. You can always get more," he mumbled into his pillow.

She used a palmful of lotion and cringed when he startled at its coolness.

"Sorry," she muttered, concentrating on the muscles in his back, trying to ignore the warmth and softness of his skin, the broad contours, the crazy thoughts that his back looked solid and mighty; that it would be protective and dependable. She bent over him, working diligently, silently.

The room filled with his moans and groans and hums of bliss. It gratified her. Finally, she was doing something to please him. And maybe, just maybe, if the massage worked the tension and pain out him, she wouldn't have to surrender to defeat. Maybe he'd feel better tomorrow and they could begin falling in love—or at least have an accommodating conversation.

"Harri," he mumbled, sounding half-asleep.

"Yes?"

"What happened?"

Her fingers faltered, but she couldn't pretend not to know what he was talking about. The subject had hung invisibly between them since he'd mentioned it in the bathroom.

Dusk was settling outside the windows and the room was cast in shadows, though there was still plenty of light to see.

She was chewing her lower lip, wondering how much he needed to know and how much she could bring herself to tell him, when he spoke again.

"Was prison so awful that you can't talk about it?"

"No. Prison was a picnic compared to the rest of it. The accusations, the lies, the trial, facing my father and the people I thought to be friends. Leaving prison was harder than being there."

"What happened?"

"Do you know what I am? What I'm educated and trained to do for a living?"

"A school teacher, I thought," he said, trying to recall. "Science, right?"

"Biology. I teach undergraduate biology at Tubow College now, but only because no one else would give me a job after I was released from prison," she told him, bowing her back as it started to cramp.

"Straddle my hips, it's easier that way," he said, numb and nonchalant.

She took in the expanse of his shoulders, the small of his back, his hips and bare legs and decided that she couldn't straddle any of it.

"Harriet, I'd have to be triple jointed to rape you from this position," he groused into his pillow. "Give yourself a break."

Leaning over the bed *was* awkward. She climbed up on him rapidly, impulsively, before she had time to give the act any more thought. "Where does it hurt the most?"

"My shoulders and neck," he said. "You didn't teach school before you went to jail, I take it."

"I'm a biochemist. I worked for a pharmaceutical company in New Jersey, in research and development."

"How long?"

"Since college. I was second in my class. I showed great promise, they said. I was there eight years, got my doctorate in pharmacology." She laughed softly. "I thought I had the world by the tail. I had almost everything I ever wanted."

"Almost?"

"Career wise, I mean. I still wanted a husband and children, but as it turned out, it was just as well I didn't have them."

"What happened?"

She laughed. "I got a big head. I thought I was smart. I believed in myself and I trusted someone." He attempted to turn his head to look at her but couldn't quite make it. "Lie still. It'll be easier to tell you, if I don't have to look at you."

"Okay."

"The first few years were great. I was part of a team working on a new, safer anticoagulant. For thromboplastic disease mostly, like for coronary patients, stroke patients, diabetics—it can be used for a variety of clotting disorders—a great drug, and in pharmaceutical circles it caused quite a stir, let me tell you." He made a noise, and she continued. "We were semicelebrities, and I was gobbling it up like a pig. I got another job offer from a company in New York, a bigger company with bigger projects and bigger pay. I gobbled that up too."

She took a deep breath and forged on.

"At first they had me doing odds and ends. Isolating and growing viruses; for a while I had a whole lab full of controls—animals that were control studies in lab experiments. All I did was feed them and clean their cages, basic stuff a lab attendant could do. It was completely beneath me," she said, being facetious now but able to recall how indignant she'd been at the time. "One great day, though, I was called upstairs to the director's office. He introduced me to Dr. Maxwell Goldtharpe. He is a brilliant scientist. He's been nominated for the Nobel Prize twice. Someday he'll win it, too, wait and see. But anyway, they had enticed him away from another company as well, and *he* wanted *me* to work with him. It was a great honor, and I was thrilled. But accepting the position was a big mistake."

"How so?"

"Max and I fell in love—well, more accurately, I guess I fell in love with Max. I respected him, admired him, thought he was a savior to mankind. And he trusted me. I got my own lab and my own project—a bacterial enzyme that we hoped would either poison or retard the growth of cancer cells."

"Must be nice, working to cure the world's ills."

"It's more like looking for cures and getting disappointed a lot when you don't find them."

"So, your big project was a dud."

"My project was a great success, except that the chemical formula used to grow and sustain the bacteria that produced the enzyme was stolen from another company."

"Max's old company?"

"It was addressed to me, and I signed for it when it arrived by special courier. The sender was conveniently unnamed, except for the name of the company. It was kept in the vault, and I was the only one to check it in and out, because I was the only one working on the project. It was kept under wraps because Max was afraid that any publicity would make it a target for theft."

"But then it got out," he suggested.

"At a Christmas party Max had been invited to by some of his old friends at the other company. He took me, and we got separated for a while. The long and the short of it is that I got stuck with a drooling drunk who started telling me about how close he and his pals were to making a breakthrough on a chemically mutated bacterial enzyme to combat cancer cells."

"Sit up a second," Payton said. She did, and before she realized what he was doing, he'd rolled onto his back. She moved to get off him, but he reached out and grabbed her wrists, pulling them down to his chest. "Pecs, too, please," he said, acting as if a woman sitting on his pelvis was a common occurrence.

Maybe it was, she thought, disturbed. Maybe he had more women than he knew what to do with already. Mr. DeLuca hadn't said much about it, other than that Payton's social activities indicated that he was heterosexual and there didn't appear to be a special relationship with any one woman. What if he loved many women and couldn't settle for one? What were his other women like? Beautiful? Charming? Not like her?

"So the other guy's project sounded familiar, right?"

"Like ten-months-of-my-life familiar," she said, kneading the muscles in his neck, chest, and upper arms. "So then, I confronted Max with what I'd heard. Another big mistake."

"Why?" he asked, watching her intently. He was neither condemning nor sympathetic, merely interested, and that made it easier to tell him.

"Max told me it was garbage. That my project must have been leaked somehow, and the man at the party was trying to get information from me or he was working on something similar by coincidence."

"And you believed him." It wasn't a question.

"Of course, I did. I had no reason not to until the police showed up to arrest me." A sad smile came to her lips. "It was decided that I had an accomplice inside Cole Pharmaceutical, who stole the formula and bacteria for me. Max's memory became amazingly selective. He could remember that I was very secretive about my project and would tell him only the bare essentials. He couldn't remember assigning me the project or any of the hundreds of conversations we had about it, only that I'd begged him to trust me with an idea I had and, of course, he being the brilliant scientist and me being very promising, he'd been willing to give me a chance to work on my own. And who do you think the jury believed?"

"The brilliant scientist, Max."

"I was convicted of industrial espionage and grand theft, and sentenced to three years in prison."

"Three years?" He frowned. "You weren't in that long."

"Eighteen months with good behavior and eighteen months probation," she said, engrossed in massaging the muscles of his left arm. "I see a probation officer every other week now, though how they expect me to go back to my wicked ways when I can't get past the reception desk of a generic drug manufacturer, I have no idea."

He laughed, and she glared at him.

"My career is ruined and you're amused?"

"Not at all," he said, looking remarkably diverted. "It's just that you don't seem as mad about it as, say, I would be. I'd be on a blood hunt."

She nodded, flinging her braid back with a toss of her head, switching to his right arm. "I was bitter. Through the trial and during the first twelve months in prison. I wanted blood. I used to lie awake at night, dreaming of ways to expose Max and destroy his life." She sat back thoughtfully, resting her hands on her thighs. "Toward the end, though, I just wanted to get out and get my life back. I was tired of defending myself, of blaming myself, of hating Max and the rest of the world as well. All I wanted was my life."

"But you lost that when they convicted you."

She looked surprised. "No, I didn't. I lost my career. Something that interested me, excited me; something I enjoyed doing, but it was never my whole life. And I still have the interest and enjoyment of what attracted me to biochemistry in the first place, in teaching."

"Then, by life you mean marriage and kids."

"I mean loving, living, learning, listening, looking, laughing." She chuckled. "All them great *L* words."

"And what was it that attracted you to biochemistry in the first place?" he asked, his hands coming to rest naturally on her forearms.

She shrugged, feeling a belated awkwardness in her position. "Biology was my first love. I'm fascinated by the way everything from one-cell organisms to man and the universe are all intricately related and interdependent. It's all held together chemically and it only takes one wrong chemical to destroy it."

"And do you like teaching it as well as researching it?" he asked, his voice gentle and caring, his hands slipping down to cover hers.

"I didn't think I would, but I do. It's a very small, undistinguished college, but I like lighting fires under my students, sparking their interest, fanning their enthusiasm and imagination."

"There's no fame or glory in it," he pointed out.

"I had more than my share during the trial." She watched his fingers entwine with hers. Understanding. Reassuring. Sensuous. "I don't need or want it in my life anymore."

He lifted their hands from her thighs and made a slow examination of the shape and size of her fingers, her nails, the way they curled around his.

"What is it you do want and need in your life, Harri?" he asked almost absently, a faraway expression softening the hard contours of his face. His gaze locked with hers.

Should she be honest or philosophical, she mused, watching him watch her.

"Someone to love," she said simply.

A wry smile twisted his perfect mouth. "And your island."

He brushed the soft skin between her thumb and index finger, dispatching a thousand prickling thrills up her arm.

"That too," she said, feeling winded, spellbound by the sensations he was creating. "But not as much."

Her eyes widened with fanciful prospects when he slowly licked his bottom lip and even more slowly pulled it through his even white teeth. Without warning, he extended his arms to their full length, taking her hands with him, crushing her chest to his chest, bringing her face to within inches of his.

"What will it feel like, Harri? How will we know when it's happening?" he asked, as breathless as she.

"What?" Her voice was a panting whisper; her heart an erratic pounding in her ears; her belly and below spiraling with excitement and expectation.

"The magic," he murmured, his breath warm against her lips. "How will we know when it's taking effect? You've been in love. What will it feel like?"

His eyes asked the same questions, profound in their need to know.

"I don't know," she said, mesmerized.

A simultaneous tug on both her arms brought her lips to his. He took her lower lip between his teeth as he had his own moments earlier. He sipped and nibbled. He flicked his tongue against her upper lip, brushed his lips across hers lightly. Openmouthed, she grazed her lips across his in the same manner. His moan of pleasure filled her empty mouth before he covered it with his.

Instinctively, the hollow void inside her sought fulfillment. Her tongue met his on equal terms, with equal need and equal promise.

His hands released hers to wander untamed over her body, to squeeze her tightly to him. She clenched fists full of dark hair, pulling him closer, sinking deeper and deeper into the kiss until he rolled her beneath him, parting her legs with his, using his knee to apply pressure to the sharpest point of her aching desire.

Hot and panting, she felt him setting stray wisps of curling hair away from her face with a tender touch. Her eyes opened to a picture of wonderment in mossy green. In his eyes she could see the amazement, the passion, and the longing that were clouding her own mind.

"We shouldn't do this," she said with a gasp, wishing she had one good reason not to.

"Too late. We're doing it," he said, his breathing rapid, his body strained with wanting as he attempted to kiss her again.

"No. This isn't right."

"Feels right to me."

"It's not. We hardly know each other."

"We know we want each other."

"That's not enough," she said, palms on his chest, pushing him away. "Mr. Dunsmore. Please."

"What?" he said, promptly pulling away as if she'd slapped him. "Mr. Dunsmore?" For a moment he looked at her as if he'd been deceived, then he rolled away to sit on the edge of the bed. "Why is it so damned difficult for you to say my name?" he asked. He turned to look at her. "Pay-ton. Say it."

"Payton."

"Good. Don't called me Mr. Dunsmore anymore," he said.

"All right," she said, casting him a wary eye from the other side of the bed.

"Thank you for your help," he said, dismissing her, unable to look at her, barely able to tolerate her presence. "I can manage from here."

"Are you sure?"

"What?" he snapped, daring her to be foolish enough to repeat the question. She circled the bed.

"Well, I . . . I'm concerned about you. I want to help."

"Then go away," he said, turning away from her.

"You should eat something."

"You should leave me be. Now."

What was she doing to him? he pondered in the silence that followed her departure from the room. Teasing and happy one minute, testy and foul-tempered the next—with no good explanation for either disposition. One instant he wanted to taste her from head to toe like a Popsicle, and the next, he wanted to get as far away from her as possible. There were times when he actually liked the woman, but at the moment he didn't trust her any farther than he could throw her with both his arms broken—and *that* made him angry because he *wanted* to trust her, get close to her, know her.

Somewhere deep within him something resented her patience and kindness, hated her uncomplaining willingness to care for him, cringed at her gentle touch.

He'd meant what he said, he didn't want her addressing him formally anymore—though why he gave a damn what she called him was totally beyond him.

His burst of temper, her passiveness, the unexpected storm of confusion and turmoil inside him, the soft scent of lilac, and an unfamiliar sensation of frustration grated his nerves raw.

He punched the pillow next to his face and squelched an urge to scream. What was happening? He didn't know the name of the game he was playing, but he knew he didn't like it. He always played for high stakes, but he sensed that they were dangerously too high this time. He never played games unless he was sure to win. He felt lost.

A chuckle gathered at the back of his throat, and a smile twisted his lips despite his furrowed brow. Dammit. Teasing and heckling Harriet Wheaton was more soul-tickling fun than anything he'd done in years. Lord! She was gullible and sweet and gentle and giving and caring and nice to look at and heaven to smell, and her kisses were like sweet, warm wine . and . . .

"Payton?" came a soft, tentative whisper.

"Hmm?" He was glad she'd come back. Elated.

"I'm leaving a little bell here beside the bed," she said timidly. "In case you need anything. And some fruit, in case you get hungry."

Aw, hell. The apprehension in her voice was like a kick in his gut. He wanted to leap up, take her into his arms, kiss her, and beg for her forgiveness. He cursed his rude tongue, and then wondered if he was losing his mind.

"You're very kind, Harriet. Thank you," he said, caught between a rock and a hard place. He wanted to hurt her again and send her away; he wanted to apologize and hold her close.

"Not at all. Please don't hesitate to call me," she said.

Then he was alone in the room once more. He sat up. She'd left the door to the walkway slightly ajar and the door to the hidden hall that led to her room wide open. He knew an odd, brief ache in his chest as he got to his feet and began to pace the room, troubled and restless.

Six

Harriet yawned and closed the last of a stack of books she'd taken from the library. She tossed it to the floor with the others beside her bed and stretched her muscles, long and leisurely. Half the night had slipped away while she fretted about Mr—.

"Payton. Payton. Payton," she muttered, determined to make the name come readily to her lips. It had been Mr. Dunsmore, her adversary, for so long that Payton, her cocastaway, seemed like an entirely different person.

Anyway, she'd brooded about him most of the night. About him, his illness, his kiss . . .

Finally, in the wee hours of the morning, she'd made an excursion to the library. Every medical book she could find agreed that sudden, intense head pain and severe mood swings could be symptoms of a hundred nasty brain ailments—and they all needed immediate attention.

She shouldn't have waited, and she wasn't going to put it off any longer, she firmly resolved. She'd get him back to St. Peter's Bay and the care he needed first thing that morning. Risking her future was one thing, risking his was something else entirely.

Her head lifted to the distant tinkle of a bell.

"Hi," she said, peering into Payton's room a minute

later, having sprinted down the hidden hall from her room, tying on her robe as she went. She smiled and he smiled back. "Are you feeling better?"

Please. Please. Please, she pleaded, walking into the room to get a better look at him.

"A bit." He looked as tired as she felt. "I'm sorry if I disturbed you. I . . . knocked the bell over."

"That's okay. I'm glad you're feeling better. Are you hungry?"

"A bit." He was sleepy-faced and scary-haired and undeniably cute. His mother must have loved him very much, she mused.

"Good. I'll get you something. I'll be right back."

"Harriet?" She turned back at the door. "What time is it?"

"About six-thirty. Has your watch stopped?"

"My . . ." He looked at the watch on his wrist as if he'd never seen it before. "Oh, I forgot."

Pain. Mood swings. Memory loss. Ah, jeez. Her heart dropped through the floor. A kiss. That was all it had been. She shouldn't have let it affect her so. She should have taken the kiss in stride and sent him back to the mainland the night before.

"Six-thirty in the morning?" he said, glancing at the windows in dismay. Couldn't he tell it was morning? she wondered and added vision disturbances to her list. "I thought it was later than that. I'm going back to sleep. You should too. It's too early to be up cooking breakfast." He burrowed into the covers, saying, "Lord, I'm tired."

Acute fatigue. Loss of appetite.

"Payton," she said, approaching the bed, hoping she hadn't waited too long; praying his condition wouldn't deteriorate any further before she could get him to a hospital. "I have an idea. I've been thinking . . ."

"Me too," he said, bracing himself on one elbow to look at her. "I was awake most of the night thinking I should apologize to you, but then I decided not to. I wanted to kiss you, I liked kissing you, and I won't say I'm sorry I did it."

"Oh, well, um," she stammered nervously, wanting to giggle despite the fact that she thought the kiss had been a side effect of his illness. "That's not what I meant. I mean, there's no need to apologize. I . . . it happened, and now I think—"

"You liked it too, right?" he said, rudely assuming he knew her mind and terribly pleased with his insights.

"Yes, of course," she said, patting his arm, placating and consoling. "And now I think—"

"It's time for more," he said, grinning, reaching out to pull her down on top of him. "Great idea."

"No. Uh-ah. No," she said, struggling. "You're putting words in my mouth. This isn't what I had in mind."

He stopped. His brows lifted in interest. He smiled licentiously and nodded.

"You're right, that's a better idea," he said, reaching for the buttons on the front of her silky pajamas.

"No," she cried. "No. That's not it either."

"What *did* you have in mind, Harri?" His voice was like century-old whiskey. Rough, potent, intoxicating. Offhand, she couldn't recall what she'd been thinking.

"Stop that," she said, pulling his hands out from under her robe and nightshirt. "What is the matter with you?"

Not one of the books had mentioned crazed sexual advances.

"I don't know," he muttered, his lips doing brain-boggling things on her neck. "Maybe I'm enchanted.

Bewitched. Spellbound. Isn't that what's supposed to happen to us here?"

She looked down into his face. "You're feeling a whole lot more than a bit better, aren't you?"

"Right now, I feel downright frisky."

"You're not ill anymore?"

He rolled over on top of her and took her hands in his.

"I never was ill," he said, and when she began to fight her way out from under him, he held tight and refused to move. "I thought that if you thought I was sick enough, you'd get us rescued."

"Well, you gave up your act too soon," she said, seething, recalling his every sickly complaint and whining request. "You'd won. I was going to send you back this morning."

"You were?"

"Yes."

"That's strange," he said. "I can usually read people pretty well. I was sure you'd wait till my head popped wide open before you called for help."

She gasped. "What a horrible thing to think of me."

"You're angry."

"Hell, yes, I'm angry. I don't like being played for a fool any more than you do," she said. "Get off of me."

"No. Not until you ask me why I changed my mind about staying and why I just told you the truth."

"Okay. Why?"

"Lay still and I'll tell you."

"Stop me and tell me," she said, though she did stop squirming.

He scanned her face before he spoke. "The acoustics in that hallway are incredible. I heard you every time you came across to check on me last night; when you left to go downstairs; when you returned. I even snuck down the hall to see what you were reading."

"So?"

"Were you worried about me because you thought I'd die and you'd go to jail again or were you really worried about me?"

"Both."

"And you're honest to a fault, aren't you?"

"I don't lie very well, so I either tell the truth or say nothing at all."

"What would you say if I told you that I wanted to try your . . . experiment, see if it really works."

"I'd ask why."

"And if I said my reasons were personal?"

"Then I'd only wonder why and hope that you'd tell me someday."

"That's it?" He looked surprised. "You wouldn't nag me to tell you?"

"No. You're entitled to your privacy."

His tongue played with his back teeth as he contemplated her. He pinched the lapel of her shirt, pulled it slowly away from her skin, and craned his neck to peek underneath.

"What else am I entitled to?" he asked, meeting her gaze with a playful smile.

"Not me," she said, slapping her hands to her chest.

"I thought that was the whole point, for me to want you."

"And vice versa," she pointed out.

"And vice versa," he agreed.

"It is. But not sexually."

"Not sexually?" He looked as if he'd just chewed and swallowed a lemon.

"Sexually, too, but later, when we know if we like each other well enough to spend more time together," she said. "Get off."

He did and watched her scramble off the bed.

"So, how do we go about this . . . this falling in love

stuff? Do we have to do something special or does the island take care of everything?"

She shrugged.

"I thought you knew all about the magic."

"All I know is the history of it. If I'd experienced it firsthand already, I wouldn't be testing it now," she said.

"True."

"And always before, it worked with chance meetings. I believe I'm the first to actually manufacture a situation in which to tempt the Fates. And we didn't really meet on the island. I'm not sure it'll work at all."

He considered these departures from the tradition. "You know, you took an incredible gamble on this. Is it really so important to you?"

She flung her braid back where it belonged and nodded.

"Why?"

Why. How could she explain intangibles such as faith and hope without sounding like a dream junkie? Looking away, she wrapped her arms around her waist and moved aimlessly about the room.

"What happened to me? The worst part of it? Was the disillusionment," she said haltingly. "I fought to prove my innocence with everything I could, and still I lost. It destroyed so many things that were very basic in me. Such as my faith in justice, in right and wrong, in love, in people . . . in me. I wasn't even too sure about God anymore. And if He did exist, I couldn't understand why He'd turned his back on me. It was hard for me to believe in anything anymore."

"You *want* to believe in the magic," he said, knowing disillusionment, familiar with the need to believe. He couldn't help but admire her perseverance, though it was probably still too early for her to realize that it would be best to simply give up and stop looking for something that didn't exist. He'd given up believing years ago.

"I do want to believe," she said, looking at him. "It sounds crazy, I know, wanting to believe in magic. But without it, I can't see any hope for my future, and without that I . . ." She shrugged and left her words hanging ominously in the air.

Payton knew the road she was on, and a twinge of protectiveness seized him. He wasn't a do-gooder, but he wanted to travel the road once more with her. He could show her the shortcuts and the pitfalls and make the inevitable destination a little less painful.

"Well," he said, taking control of the situation. "We need a place to start. As I see it, we can A: Go back to the beach and pretend to start all over. B: Continue on from here with more philosophical discussions. Or C: Jump back in the sack together—my personal choice—giving us a common base on which to build a relationship, if the magic works."

"Do you always talk like that?"

"Like what? Logically?"

"Like everything is cut-and-dried, right or left, up or down. Period. Is everything a multiple choice question to you?"

"Pretty much. Yes."

"Okay," she said, having a somewhat analytical mind herself. "You forgot D."

"D?"

"D: We separate now to shower and dress, and we meet in the kitchen in thirty minutes to start all over again with breakfast. We'll have philosophical discussions and common conversations." She grinned the grin of a siren. "And fantasize about jumping into the sack together while we're getting acquainted."

Payton released a resigned sigh and frowned his disapproval.

"You're one of those women who do everything the hard way, aren't you?"

She laughed as she walked to the door. "It seems like it, doesn't it?"

Payton took longer than the allotted thirty minutes to get to the kitchen. The suitcase of clothes turned out to be an amazingly well-thought-out project, that was one surprise after another. Aside from the pajamas, it was a tasteful collection of casual clothes and a cache of male essentials from his favorite cologne to multiple vitamins. She and her friend DeLuca had left no stone unturned and no prospect neglected.

One of the first things he planned to do when he got off the island was to have a long talk with Mr. DeLuca—after that, he might consider putting the man on his payroll.

He remained uncertain of his impulse to join Harriet in her impossible quest. And he wasn't sure why he was looking forward to the undertaking. To him, love and happily ever after were like pablum for babies, filling their bellies, luring them into a false sense of security that would later be shattered when they discovered that the true way of the world was uncertain and fraught with hunger and starvation.

Still, the idea of looking for love intrigued him. It wasn't as though he believed in the existence of such a fine human emotion, but Harriet's antics appealed to him the way some people were enthralled by psychic phenomena. Could she be real or was she a fascinating hoax?

"My stomach is an extremely vulnerable part of my anatomy," he said, entering the kitchen, fairly bowled

DON'T HOLD BACK!

1. No obligation! No purchase necessary! Enter our Sweepstakes for a chance to win!
2. FREE! Get your first shipment of 6 Loveswept books *and* a lighted makeup case as a free gift.
3. Save money! Become a member and about once a month you get 6 books for the price of 5! Return any shipment you don't want.
4. Be the first! You'll always receive your Loveswept books before they are available in stores. You'll be the first to thrill to these exciting new stories.

Give in to love and see where passion leads you!
Enter the Winners Classic Sweepstakes and
send for your FREE lighted makeup case and
6 FREE Loveswept books today!

(See details inside.)

Detach here and mail today.

over by the breakfast aroma that met him. "If what you're cooking tastes half as good as it smells, I'll declare defeat and marry you this afternoon."

"Declare defeat?" she asked, glancing over her shoulder at him. "Listen mister, I happen to be a great cook. And if you're very, very nice to me, I might let you beg me to make lunch for you later."

"Oh, great," he said with a groan, swinging a leg over a stool at the work island. "A libber."

"No. Not really. Just a woman who wants a little respect."

He smirked at the back of her head, his eyes automatically lowering to the tight, round curves of her denim-covered bottom.

"I hope we're not about to have our first philosophical discussion," he said. "Philosophy bores me."

"Then behave," she said, her tone light. "Do you know how to make toast?"

"Sure. Order it from room service."

"Is that a joke?"

"Nope," he said, standing to join her on the other side of the work bar. "Both my parents had housekeepers to cook toast. At school we got it in the cafeteria, and now I either eat out or order room service. Educate me."

She looked at him, a thousand questions crowding her mind.

"See that little boxlike thing over there, with the slits in the top?" He walked over to scrutinize the toaster with much ado. "Drop a piece of bread in each slot, push the lever on the side down until it sticks, and when the bread pops up, butter it. You can butter bread, can't you?"

His expression was vapid. "Like . . . with a knife?"

"That's right." A smile tugged at her lips when he pushed up the sleeves of his sweater and looked as if he were about to create gourmet toast. "If both your parents had housekeepers, should I assume that they were divorced?"

"Terminally divorced. They hated each other," he said, squinting into the toaster to watch the bread turn golden brown. He was conscious of the ease with which his statement had come, yet he rarely spoke of his family.

"That must have been hard for you," she said.

"That was the way it was," he said casually. "My family's legacy is a little different than yours. Dunsmores are doomed to divorce, you might say."

"Were you ever married?"

"Sure. And divorced. Luckily, I was quick to get the message."

"What message?"

"Not to marry again." The toast popped up, and he glanced at her for approval. The concern in her eyes surprised him. "Relax. It isn't unheard of for a Dunsmore to think he's in love again, and to remarry over and over again. As a matter of fact, each of my father's divorces has resulted in a trip to the Bahamas, and he invariably returns married to someone else. I have a half sister who cleans out her closets, loses twenty pounds, and buys an entirely new wardrobe before she goes husband hunting again. She's done that three times so far. One of my stepbrothers drank himself stupid after his first divorce and then he eloped with an exotic dancer who was already married to someone else. My mother married twice before she discovered that husbands were more aggravation than pleasure and that disposable lovers were the way to go."

"And you?"

He'd spent the past ten years devoted to his work, and feeling as hard and cold as his ex-wife accused him of being, but for Harriet's edification, he said, "I made a life of my own. The only person I trust is me. The only person I care about is me. I don't own anything I can't afford to lose, and there's no one in my life that I'd miss if they were gone tomorrow."

She had filled two plates with thick slices of Canadian bacon and light, fluffy scrambled eggs but arrested all movement to stare at him.

"I don't believe you," she said, sensing he wasn't quite as cavalier on the subject as he sounded. "You're not at all like that."

"How the hell would you know?" he asked, dumbfounded. "And if you tell me your friend DeLuca told you anything different than what I'm telling you, then you were a chump for hiring him, because he doesn't know what he's talking about either."

She put the fry pan in the sink and took up the plates. "I don't need Mr. DeLuca to tell me that you're not a very nice man. But I don't believe you're as indifferent and heartless as you'd like me to think."

"Why not?"

Intuition? she speculated, looking at him. She set his plate on the table across from her and reached to pour them both some coffee.

"Your eyes."

"My eyes?" He handed her two pieces of buttered toast, and sat down with two pieces for himself. "Give me a break."

"No. It's true. You're very good at hiding what you think, but when you're feeling and *not* thinking, it shows in your eyes. Like, when you think something's funny or when . . ." When he was aroused? Better not bring that up, she decided in a split second. " . . . actually, it was one of the first things I noticed about you."

"What else do you think you've noticed about me?" he asked, immeasurably curious.

"Well, you like to be in control. You're bossy and stubborn and lie without conscience, whenever it suits you—a talent I admire, by the way," she said, pausing to chew her food. "You're sarcastic and mean, but I don't think it comes naturally to you. I think you work at being nasty."

He laughed. "And why would I do that?"

"To survive," she said. Her eyes met his, deep and knowing.

His smile faded, and he broke eye contact before she could see anything else she wasn't supposed to see.

"It's going to rain," he complained sometime later. "Look at that sky."

She laughed and handed the coat back to him. "That sky will get a lot darker before the storm breaks. We have plenty of time for a walk." She opened the kitchen door. "Just suck in some of that clean fresh air."

"I knew the minute I saw you that you were a nature freak," he grumbled, hauling on the thick deerskin jacket she'd scrounged up for him. "Breathing the air, saving the fish, picketing furriers. I bet you plant a tree every Arbor Day."

"Not just on Arbor Day," she said, tugging on his sleeve to move him out into the brisk wind. "The Wheaton side of my family had traditions too. From the time I was born, my dad added an apple sapling to the orchard every year on my birthday. That tree over there is a red maple they planted to celebrate one of their wedding anniversaries. Every year it was a different kind of tree—but no oaks."

"Why not?"

"I'll show you."

They walked west, toward the cliffs that faced Ontario. She showed him a small clearing in the dense woods where one of the brides had cultivated a private rock garden, where on warm summer days Harriet often came to catch the breezes, relax, and do a little daydreaming on the loveseat beneath a canopy of green leaves.

For a short distance she guided him across the top of the ridge. The jagged rock wall and boulders below, pounded by wave after wave after wave, with no beginning and no end, was one of her most favorite sights on the island. It brought a green cast to Payton's complexion, however, so she didn't tarry long.

At last they came to an open space, a clearing, sheltered from the bitter northwest winds by an outcrop of rock twenty or thirty feet high.

"These are oaks. They're slow growing, very strong, very hardy trees. By the time they outgrow that wall of rock there, they'll be able to withstand almost anything," she said, motioning to two sleeping young giants, one several years older and larger than the other. She put the palm of her hand to the trunk of the tree. "My father planted this one when my mother died. They'd agreed on it ahead of time, thinking it would give whoever was left something to do, rather than sitting around feeling sad."

Payton looked at the smaller tree, several yards away.

"You planted that one when your father died," he said, knowing it as sure as he knew that if she looked at him in that moment, he'd see tears in her eyes.

She stepped across to the smaller tree and removed a lone dead leaf from its branches. "It was a while before I got a chance to plant it for him. I . . . he died while I was still in prison."

"I'm sorry," he said, feeling a deep stab of profound sadness. For a man he'd never met? Or for her?

She looked at him, as if from a faraway place, and then she smiled a smile that was sweeter than anything he'd tasted; sharper than anything he'd touched; wiser than anything he'd heard.

"Careful," she said. "You sound sincere. I'll start thinking you're more than half-human and not such a bad guy after all, if you don't watch your step."

"Heaven forbid," he said, suspecting that she felt as awkward accepting his sympathy as he was feeling giving it. "We can't have that. The mystic forces will think they've done it again, if we start talking as if we like each other."

If, indeed, there were mystic forces on the island, they were no doubt laughing up their sleeves at that moment, Harriet mused. For the truth of the matter was, she walked away from the new oaks laughing; basking in the glow of unquestioned camaraderie, something that couldn't exist without mutual support and acceptance.

Seven

"I know ten politicians who, *together,* don't cheat as much as you do," Payton complained, racking the balls on the pool table for a fifth and last game.

"Name them," she said, smirking at his testiness.

He gave it a go. "Bob Weaver."

"Never heard of him."

"He's a young councilman, very into education and civil liberties. I met him at one of my mother's parties last year, and she swears that he's as straight as a ruler."

"Your mother's politically active?"

"Not hardly," he said, lining up his shot behind the cue-ball.

"Then how can she be a judge of this man's integrity?"

"Given my mother's penchant for young men, there are other ways to test a man's integrity." He pocketed a solid-colored ball and left the stripes for Harriet.

"Okay. I'll take your word for it, but that still leaves nine more," she said smugly, feeling playful.

"Let me think," he said, considering his next move. After a few seconds he reluctantly admitted to being stymied. "Do you expect me to remember the names of every politician I meet?"

"A big real estate wheeler-dealer like you? Yes," she said, a challenge in her voice. "You remember all the names. You just can't connect any of them with an honest man, is all."

He narrowed his eyes at her and prepared to do battle, then thought better of it. "Politicians were a bad association, *but* if I had my Rolodex, I could list the names of a hundred men who'd rather die than cheat at pool."

"How can you cheat at pool?" she asked, pooh-poohing his grievance. "I've been playing pool since I was a little girl, and short of dropping the balls into the pockets by hand or tilting the table, you can't cheat at it. Why can't you admit that you're intimidated by my *skill?*"

"Skill, hell," he said, stopping midshot to gape at her. "You took your foot a good six inches off the floor. You were practically laying on the table."

"I was not. I admit I was stretching for the shot, but I didn't take my foot off the floor. Frankly, I've always thought that when one person is taller than the other, there ought to be a handicap imposed on the game."

"A handicap." He was terribly amused. Only a woman would want to handicap a game of pool.

"Yes," she said vehemently, but grinning. "They do it for other games, like golf and bowling. I think if you're taller, I should get the difference between us in inches."

"Sounds good to me," he said, and before she could blink twice, he had her flat on her back on the pool table and was hoisting his leg up to join her.

"What are you doing?" she shrieked, when a big hand on her chest foiled her attempts to sit up.

"Lay still. I am attempting to calibrate the difference between us in inches," he said, spanning her body with his, aligning his pelvis to hers.

His weight, his warmth, his musky male odor were overwhelming. His hands on her wrists were scorching. It hurt to breathe.

"But is this really necessary? Couldn't you simply ask me how tall I am and subtract the difference from your height?"

"I could, but it wouldn't be as much fun," he said, making a big to-do of wiggling atop her and looking down the lengths of their bodies for accuracy. Finally, he became very still, looking down into her face with a distinct light in his eyes. "I think the difference between us is a good stiff seven inches or so. And I sure wouldn't mind handicapping you with that much of the dissimilarity between us."

She gasped at his double entendre, and then she sputtered into a fit of laughter.

Patiently, and without concealing the effort it was costing him, he held her wrists and waited for her self-control to return.

"It was a serious offer, Harriet," he said when she'd calmed to titters and giggles. "And I must say that your behavior shows a decided lack of good sportsmanship."

She snorted once and was howling again while he fought the smile that was threatening to take over his lips. Oddly, he was acquiring a predilection for the sound of her laughter—a happy, joyous sound that seemed to heat cold, empty places in his heart. With his index finger, he gently wiped away a tear escaping from the corner of her eye.

She stiffened.

"Oh, please," she cried, weak with merriment. "Get off. I'm going to wet my pants."

"On great-great-grandpa's pool table?"

"Buckets," she wailed. "Oh, please."

Her squirming told him it wasn't another one of her tricks, and he hastily jumped to the floor. He helped her up and grinned when she skirted away. He called after her, "You cheat at pool. You're not a good sport. You can't hold your water, and you have no respect for antiques. These things do not augur a happily-ever-after ending for us, Harriet."

"Payton?" she called, returning several minutes later to find the billiard room empty. She walked across the hall to the library and discovered him slouched in a chair before the fire they'd started earlier. It was now dying. "That was a real slick trick you pulled to get out of losing another game to me."

He put on a marvelous mask of dismay. "It was supposed to be a slick seduction."

Taking the chair next to his, she smiled. "It was that too."

"So, what do we have to do before we can have sex? Dance naked on the beach? Draw blood? What?" he asked, referring to the island's mysterious powers.

"Maybe when it becomes more than just sex."

"Ah. The sexual nomenclature syndrome and the vast gray area between having sex and making love."

"Don't you think there's a difference?"

He rolled his head against the back of the chair to look at her. He studied her long and hard before saying, "There's a difference."

"Did you have sex or make love to your wife?" The question was out before she could stop it. "I'm sorry. That's none of my business."

Whether it concerned her or not; whether it was because she was a relative stranger, a temporary entity in his life, or whether it was because he was comfortable with her and didn't feel threatened by her, he wanted to tell her.

"I made love and she tolerated it," he said, watching the fading embers of the fire. "Barely."

Well, in for a penny . . .

"She, ah, didn't like it?" she asked.

"She didn't like me." When Harriet remained silent, he glanced at her. He could sense all the questions on her mind and her reluctance to ask them, but more than that he felt not sympathy or pity from her, but an empathy and understanding that made it easier for him to continue. "Do you believe in perfect people, Harri?"

"No."

He smiled. "Good. I knew you wouldn't. But there are people who do, you know. My parents, the people I grew up with, the exclusive society I was brought up in." He looked away. "I believed. I was Payton Augustus Dunsmore IV, and the spoon in my mouth wasn't silver, it was gold. I grew up with all the privileges and advantages; the perfect parents, the perfect schools, never questioning, never rocking the boat. I knew all the right people and did all the right things because it was expected of me, the perfect boy."

"Only . . . I wasn't the perfect boy. I believed in perfect, and I worked hard at being perfect. I got good at convincing other people that I was perfect, and that everything around me was perfect. Sometimes I could even fool myself. But I didn't feel perfect. Not the way I thought I should feel." He paused, frowning. "I mean, here I had these perfect parents. They were divorced, but they both had big, fine homes I could sleep in, they both left money with the housekeepers for me. All I had to do was ask for it. My parents paid to send me to the best schools, and in the summertime I went to the best camps. They introduced me to the children of all their best friends. I had the best clothes, the best toys, the best of everything. I was heir to their perfect world, and I hated them . . . for everything."

He stood, bent to throw a few stray wood chips into the fire, then braced one arm on the mantel. "Actually, I didn't always hate them. I don't hate them now. I resent them and I feel sorry for them, but . . . I used to think it was me. I used to think that if my parents were perfect and the world I lived in was perfect, then I was the imperfection. Because I was scared and lonely at school. I didn't enjoy camp. I felt sick inside when no one showed up to see anything I did. I was hurt when no one came on parents' day, and I was angry when the chauffeur picked me up on the last day of school, with packed suitcases, and took me straight to camp. If I were as perfect as I should have been, I wouldn't have felt like that. I wouldn't have minded the fact that the only time I saw my father was to meet a new stepmother or that I saw my mother once a day on the rare occasions I was home. If I were perfect, it wouldn't have mattered."

"Still," he held up a finger and glanced at her, "knowing I was basically imperfect, flawed to the bone, it didn't stop me from striving for perfection. I never told anyone how I felt or showed it in any way. I got good grades, played a variety of sports, made friends, went to parties, grew up. And when the time, the perfect time came for me to marry, I dutifully fell in love with a girl who everyone said was perfect for me."

"But you didn't really love her," Harriet surmised, her voice soft and discerning.

He looked at her, frowning as he recalled his feelings at the time. "No. I think I really did love her," he said, sitting in his chair, half-turned toward her.

"I had feelings for her, but maybe it was only hope. I think I hoped it was love; hoped she'd be whatever was missing in me to make my life as perfect as it was supposed to be. I hoped she'd be someone I could talk to, someone I could be with, someone of my own and I wouldn't be lonely anymore." He half laughed. "I even hoped we'd have children together. Only I was going to raise them the way I'd heard other children were raised. They were going to come home after school every day, and they could only go to camp for a week in the summer, and then only if they wanted to. And they . . . well, their perfect world was going to be different than mine was."

"But you didn't have children?" she asked.

"Ha. I hardly had a marriage." He looked away. "We were married two years before I found out she was having affairs. I didn't even ask when they'd started, it was enough to know that they existed and that she wasn't mine alone." He was silent for a moment. "I don't know. She said everyone had affairs and was surprised to learn that I hadn't. She said I was naive and possessive and completely out of touch with the rest of the world. She couldn't figure out who I thought I was that I could ask for that kind of devotion and fidelity from her, when if it hadn't been for my money—my family's money really—she wouldn't have married me in the first place. She said I was boring and coldhearted."

Harriet waited, but apparently there was no more story to tell. She guessed the rest from what he'd already told her and felt a crushing pressure in her chest, squeezing her heart painfully. She wanted to reach out and touch him. She wanted to kiss away his pain, the way she would a child with a boo-boo, and make everything right for him.

"No comment?" he asked from a distance greater than the few feet that separated them physically.

"No," she replied, intuitively knowing that anything she said would have been wrong, that he'd wanted her to know his history but that he didn't want or need her opinion of it.

He looked away, and she watched the tension ease from his shoulders. Her heart smiled. Telling her had cost him. It was a gift she would treasure all her life, whether she saw him again after Sunday or not. She was touched and humbled that he'd felt safe enough in her presence to expose his secrets.

Abruptly, he stood and positioned the wire screen before the fireplace. "Do we at least get to kiss good night at this stage of our enchantment?"

"We've kissed before and nothing happened," she said, anticipating the pleasure of kissing him again.

"What do you mean, nothing happened? You didn't feel the earth shake? You didn't hear the angels singing? I could have sworn you were experiencing something."

"I did . . . I mean, I . . . ," she stammered, growing red in the face. "I mean, we kissed, and we weren't struck by lightning or anything. I . . . it seems like an okay thing for us to do. . . . Kissing."

"You think so?" he asked, a slow smile infecting his expression. She nodded, hoping she didn't look too eager to kiss him again. He took her hand and brought her to her feet in front of him. Amused, his eyes shining, his touch warm, he took on a husbandly affect and asked, "Is the cat out and the back door locked, dear?"

"What cat?"

"It's been a good day," he said, wrapping an arm around her waist with an air of ownership. "But a long one. I think it's time we . . . go up . . . to bed."

"To bed?"

He grinned. "Now, don't tell me you're reconsidering your decision to sleep in separate bedrooms? You know, I never did approve of that idea." He wagged his finger in her face and started up the stairs. "The choice is entirely yours, my dear. Though, you must know, you're more than welcome in my bed."

"Thank you, ah, dear." Not the actor he was, she giggled. "But I feel that perhaps this time apart from each other will be good for us."

She wasn't any good at improvisations either. She'd have given anything to be witty enough to ad-lib a clever line that was as seductive and unsettling as his.

"Ah, yes," he said sagely, swinging his empty arm wide. "Abstinence makes the heart grow horny. Interesting theory, that."

"I believe it's *absence* makes the heart grow *fonder*, dear."

"Actually, it's absence makes the heart grow fonder for someone *else, dear,* but let us not quibble. You're the only woman within safe walking distance of my bed. You're the one I want in it."

She gasped, and he chortled gleefully, thinking he'd made a wonderful joke. In fact, she felt that he'd probably spoken the truth. She *was* the only woman around. The only one for him to tease and flirt with, the only one he could use to satisfy his sexual needs. His if-you-can't-beat-'em-join-'em attitude was much more tolerable than his sickly complaints and his sarcastic anger, but if he thought that was all it took to join with *her,* he was very much mistaken.

"How very romantic," she said, her voice biting as she stepped out of the circle of his arm. *"Dear."*

He stopped on the stairs to stare at her.

"Whoa, Harri," he said, racing to catch up with her, leaning forward to see her face. "What's this? Did I hit a nerve? Are you romantic, Harri?"

"Don't be ridiculous," she said, feeling strange and stupid. "I'm a scientist. Chemistry. Biology. Mental and emotional compatibility. That's romance."

"This from a woman who believes in magic?" He shook his head. "Won't fly, Harri. You're a dreamer, an idealist, a hopeless romantic."

"I don't believe in the magic," she said, blurting her words. "Well, I do, but I don't. I—"

"Want to believe," he finished for her, "And that makes you a romantic."

"Okay," she said, miffed, turning on him at the top of the stairway. "All right. So I'm a little bit romantic. So what?"

"So nothing," he said softly, slowly taking the last few steps toward her, stopping only when he could feel her breath on his lips. It was a fatuity for sure, but he was vitally glad that after all she'd experienced she was still everything he'd accused her of being. A dreamer. An idealist. A romantic. He wanted so much to kiss her that he could taste her, long before he covered her mouth with his.

It was like rushing to take the last seat on a roller-coaster ride as it pulled away from the loading dock—with no time to sit down, no time to secure the safety belt, no time to catch her breath before it began its ascent. Higher and higher she went, feeling safe and secure until the pace slowed, peaked, and sent her plunging out of control, plummeting toward the unknown, falling and frantic and deliriously delighted with the thrill of it all.

Her body raced to keep up with her senses, but in vain. And when at last the ride abruptly bottomed out, she was numb, limp, euphoric.

Payton licked the last drop of dew from her sweet, soft lips before he lifted his head and opened his eyes. He held her close until she could pry her lazy eyelids apart, then smiled at her dazed expression.

"That felt like magic to me," he said. Nodding encouragingly, he added, "I think the powers that be are trying to tell us that they want us to . . . carry on, so to speak. A little more kissing, some heavy-duty petting and who knows what they might tell us to do after that?"

His eagerness brushed against something in the back of her mind, and she laughed weakly, dropping her head to his chest for support.

"We hardly know each other," she said. "Yesterday you hated me."

"I didn't hate you. I thought you were crazy," he said, then tilting her chin upward so he could look into the dark depths of her eyes, he added, "And you can tell me everything I need to know about you by answering one question."

She stepped away, putting several feet of railing between them. "No. I won't sell you my island. Not willingly. Not before Sunday."

"It doesn't have to do with the island. It's a hypo-thetical question."

She grinned. "My favorite. What is it?"

"If I told you I was afraid—terrified—of the dark, would you leave the light in the hallway on and your bedroom door open?"

Hmm. Was it a trick question? Did he have some witty, suggestive comment to make, whichever way she answered? What kind of an answer did he want? The truth or not?

"Are you afraid of the dark?" she asked, watching him.

"No." His answer was as candid as his gaze.

"Then why . . . ?"

"It's just a question."

Her brows rose in the manner he so enjoyed and she shrugged.

"Then, of course, I'd leave the light on and the door open. It would be cruel not to."

"I knew you would," he said, his voice soft and filled with emotion—something she hadn't expected. He smiled his good night to her and took the opposite direction, heading for his bedroom.

Was that it? No more sweet talk? No more soft looks? No more seduction? She had declined his proposition, but his easy acquiescence was disappointing.

"Good night, Payton," she said, her voice echoing in the vast space above the open foyer.

"Sleep well, Harriet," he said from his door on the other side of the walkway. She was about to enter her room when his voice stopped her. "Will you leave your hall door open? Please?"

Perplexed, she asked him a hundred questions with her eyes and received only fragmentary replies. His request wasn't as simple as it sounded. There was no sexual connotation, he wasn't asking her to trust him not to use it during the night. It was more a . . . a test. Yes, a test, to determine *her* trustworthiness. Not sexually—they both knew she wouldn't sneak across the hidden hallway and attack him in the middle of the night. It was more than that. It was a could-he-depend-on-her-trustworthiness test. If he called out to her, would she come? If he needed to talk, would she listen? If he was lonely, would she be there to hold him? If he wanted to cry, would she let him?

He was waiting for her answer, his expression unreadable.

"Sure. No problem," she said.

They entered different rooms, private and secluded, separated on one side by an entire house; close and intimate, conveniently connected on the other side by a shallow, soundless hallway.

Eight

For the next two days the doors at both ends of the hall between the master bedroom and the nursery stood open, and unused.

It was a time that tried a man's soul—and a woman's.

Nights were the worst. The ready gateway was the last image in Harriet's mind when she turned out the lights to sleep. It called to her in whispers. Her eyes would open to the darkness, and she would know that the door stood open, tempting and inviting. Her ears would strain to hear him breathing. Intuition teased her with the whim that his bed was warmer, and she would shiver with cold. Dozing once more, she dreamed of floating down the corridor in a long white pristine gown, hair knotted with a satin ribbon, her cheeks flushed. She was virginal, pure and absolute in her desire to be with him.

From the other end of the passageway, in Payton's dreams, he would see her coming to him. Dark hair, loose and flowing down her back and arms. Skimpy silk frills, cut high and low on her body, clinging precariously. Bare legs, long and graceful. Cheeks flushed, she was wild, wanton, and willful in her lust to be with him. His eyes would open to the darkness, and he would know that the door stood open, tempting and inviting. His ears would strain to hear her breathing. Experience teased him with the certainty that her bed was warmer, and he would shiver with cold.

"I thought you wanted me to tell you something fascinating," she complained, pushing at her glasses with the back of her hand, frowning at him.

"I did. This isn't," he said, shifting in his squat position, his leg muscles cramping.

"It is fascinating, so pay attention. I'm going to quiz you on it later."

He watched the crazy curls around her face flutter in the wind and wondered how he could have ever wished them restrained. He took in the thick, dark plait resting on her shoulder and couldn't resist the vision of what she might look like with her hair loose, wavy, tumbling over the soft curves of her body—her naked body. . . .

"This is a perfect example of the island's development. The rock, the moss, the vegetation," she said, hunkered down beside him, brushing her hands across the rocks. A solitary tern flew overhead, passing low as if to investigate the lesson. "Most of the islands are granite hilltops—a billion-year-old-Precambrian rock—flooded six thousand years ago after the last ice age. The barren rock was colonized by lichens, and as soil developed, moss grew, then grass, then shrubs, and finally the trees."

She stood and scrambled over the rocks, taking no notice of the pounding waves below. . . . at least, not the notice Payton was taking in them. Vertigo was a good word for what he was experiencing.

He hurried to catch up with her.

"Now the fascinating part," she said, as she waited for him to join her on the path that encircled the entire island, that would take them high atop the rocky cliffs for a breathtaking view of the waterway or low along the boulders at the water's edge, " . . . is that the hot, dry, southwest slopes, exposed to sun and wind, create a climate typical of latitudes much farther south, thus the southern hardwoods. But the protected northeast slopes are cool, moist, and shaded, allowing northern plants and coniferous trees to prosper. This is a phenomenon called microclimate, and it's what maintains the islands' remarkable variety of flora and fauna."

"Fascinating." More fascinating was the way the frail winter sunshine seemed to catch and shine in the depths of her eyes.

Ignoring or perhaps not even hearing his sarcasm, she went on with great verve. "I've always thought so. The deer, the wild turkeys, the snakes, turtles, birds . . . it's all so intricately balanced and—"

"Enough," he said, breaking in on her tribute to nature, taking her hand and turning her to face him. "I've been in your biology class for hours now, and I'll admit it's interesting, but it doesn't fascinate me."

"At breakfast I asked what you wanted to do today and you told me you'd leave it to me, to fascinate you. I'm doing my best."

"Do better. Tell me something about you."

"Me? I'm not fascinating. Unless you find someone who's been to jail fascinating, and I've already told you about that," she said, turning away from his piercing gaze to continue their walk, making no effort to remove her hand from his.

He wasn't ready to move on. He tightened his grip and pulled her back to face him again.

"Harriet Wheaton, you're as wild and unpredictable as these curls when they blow in the wind," he said, indulging his fondness for them with a gentle touch. "I want to know all about you."

She laughed. "You do know all about me. I've told you my family history, my history. There's nothing left to tell."

"Tell me a secret. Tell me something about you that isn't part of a public record, that no one else knows, only you."

"A secret?" She had none. Up until she'd gone to prison, her life had been terribly ordinary. A happy childhood, an awkward adolescence, college, career, jail, picking up the pieces of her life, and another career. But no real secrets.

"It can be just a thought," he said. "A thought you've never spoken aloud."

Ah, she had lots of those.

"Come on," she said, pulling at him. "I'll show you a secret thought."

Chill winds blew in their faces and rolled dark clouds across the sky. There was more scrambling over rocks, but Payton didn't mind, it was an easy downhill slope toward the water in the bay, near the dock and the boat house.

"Gosh. I haven't thought about this in years, until now. I wonder if it's still there," she said, careful of her footing on the slick surfaces.

"What?"

"Come on. If it's still here, it'll be right over . . . Yes. There. Look."

He did and saw nothing but rock and water. He watched as she jumped a tide pool and stepped up against a huge wall of stone beyond the normal waterline.

"Look there," she said, smiling. "It's still here. I did that when I was thirteen."

He couldn't comment on what he couldn't see. He put his hands on her shoulders from behind and leaned closer. There, rubbed in the rock, were the letters *HMW*.

"Harriet . . ." he started.

"Martha."

"Wheaton." He chuckled. "Your folks really had a thing for old names, didn't they? Too bad you didn't have any sisters to share them with."

"They're family names. That's why I did that," she said, nodding to the crude marks in the rock. "I hated my name. I hated all the family history and being part of something I didn't really have anything to do with and that I couldn't get away from." She paused. "Actually, I just hated being thirteen and not being anyone special, just part of a line. I wanted to make my mark, so to speak. I wanted to let the world know somehow that I was here."

"Even then, all this was a responsibility," he said, almost to himself.

"Always."

"Then why not sell it? Get out from under it. It could be your contribution to the island's history." He could hear it already. "Jovette Island was sold, late in the twentieth century, by Harriet Martha Wheaton, whose mother was the last Jovette."

"You still don't get it, do you?" she asked, realizing that her position in life wasn't a common one. "This place isn't mine to sell. It doesn't matter what my last name is, it could be Jovette and it still wouldn't belong to me. It's not like the orchard or my car or the house in Massena. They belong to me and I can sell them. But for the brief span of my lifetime this place is only in my keeping, it belongs to the Jovettes, all those before and all those after me."

He studied her thoughtfully, trying to imagine her

sense of infinity. What would it be like to be a part of something that always was and always would be? He'd always compared his own life to that of a comet, a solitary star with no orbit, streaking through the sky for a short time. And when it burnt out, it was gone forever and forgotten.

Continuity was another dream he'd given up. Children. Grandchildren. It had seemed to him that it was more important to get from one day to the next as painlessly as possible, than to worry about living forever. How could he nurture and protect a child when it took everything he had to nurture and protect himself?

Still, he could see how important it was to Harriet.

"I must be losing my mind," he said suddenly, and more to the world at large than to her.

She looked at him. "And you're just now taking notice?" she asked, grinning.

He was serious. In a silent fit of madness, he said, "You should sell some of the antiques in the house. The first editions in the library alone would pay the back taxes on this place. The attic's a gold mine, and you'd never miss a lot of that stuff. Sell it."

A tremor passed through his body, his hands trembled. Relief, shock, courage, weakness? He wasn't sure what he was feeling, only that it wasn't planned and that it had shaken him to the core.

Harriet could only stare, baffled and curious. Did he know what he'd done, or *was* he losing his mind?

He had turned and was looking out over the water when Harriet stepped in front of him, looped her arms around his neck, and stretched on tiptoe to kiss him.

He accepted her gift of appreciation with a shyness neither of them expected. Inept in the presence of true affection and admiration, he permitted the modest declaration, then stepped away from her, sorely ill at ease.

But Harriet wouldn't let go. In that microsecond she knew she'd never be able to let go of him. Like a primed siphon, her heart felt the emptiness in his and began to pour forth her love, wanting to fill all the dents, hollows, and punctures that had drained him of his hopes and dreams and of his trust.

She locked her lips to his and kissed him with a passion that bowled them both over.

What could he do?

Payton removed her glasses, slowly, carefully, deliberately. Then he wrapped his arms around her and held on tight. He followed her into oblivion and joined her in a celebration of sensation. The earth lost its trajectory, falling, dropping closer and closer to the center of the galaxy. Their bodies burned like the fires of the sun, melting away thought and memory.

She grew weak in his arms, and when the heat threatened to overtake him as well, they sank slowly to the cool, smooth stones and continued to stoke an inferno that Sol himself would have admired.

"Payton," she murmured against his lips, expecting no answer, simply speaking his name in wonderment. She had never known such needs—to give, to take, to fill and be fulfilled. She had never known such urgency—to touch, to feel. She had never known such a rightness as she felt loving Payton.

"Hmm?" He pulled his lips from hers, then returned twice more before he was ready to pay attention to what she had to say. "What?"

"Nothing. Just Payton."

Humor sparked through the haze of passion in his eyes, and he took on a sappy sort of smile.

"I'm really tempted to see what you'd do if I suggest you sell your beautiful boat too," he said, his fingers toying with the dark wispy curls that he was coming to think of as his own private pleasure. When she laughed, he looked back into the fathomless mysteries that were her eyes—they were bright and happy. "I wouldn't complain if you did it again, but . . . why did you kiss me like that?"

"You needed to be kissed."

"Why?"

"Because you did something that was very sweet and very kind and very much part of your nature, and it scared you."

He felt naked and vulnerable, and it angered him that she could make him feel that way. He gave her glasses back to her. Then, turning from her, he sat up and watched the water curl up onto the rocks, wash over the sides, then slip back into the river.

"Don't start pretending to see things in me that aren't there, Harri," he said, his voice gentle and soft, his warning blunt and hard. "I pointed out an obvious solution to your money problems, that's all. I figured you'd have spotted it sooner or later yourself. But sooner would get us rescued quicker."

So much pride, she thought, her heart swelling and aching to the point of bursting with her love for him. How horribly he must have been hurt to be at such incredible odds with himself.

"Well, whatever your motives for telling me, it was a nice thing to do, and I appreciate it," she said, carefully sidestepping his dignity. "But selling the island piece by piece is out of the question."

Payton wanted to scream and yell at her. Instead, he looked at her and calmly asked, "Why?"

She growled and shook her fists in frustration. "It's not mine to sell," she repeated. "The first editions

belonged to my grandfather and his father and his
father. . . . Certain pieces of furniture belonged to my
grandmother, other pieces to my great-grandmother
and still others to my great-great-grandmother.
There isn't one stick of furniture or a book or a
picture or a knickknack outside those in my bedroom
that are truly mine to sell. It all belongs to the house;
to its past and to future generations."

"But what if you lose it all?"

"Then I'll lose it all," she said, prepared to accept
that fate but not willing to surrender to it.

"You can't maintain a place like this on a teacher's
salary, Harriet," he said, combing an agitated hand
through his hair before he looked at her.

"I could if I sold the orchard." She folded her arms
across her bent knees and rested her cheek on them.
"If it weren't for the orchard, I wouldn't be in the mess
I'm in now. Well, maybe. I don't know. It was one of
those things that seemed right at the time, and then
it turned out all wrong."

"Sounds cosmic to me," he muttered dryly.

Maybe it was—the thought flickered briefly
through her mind. After all, would she be sitting
on the beach with Payton Augustus Dunsmore IV,
falling hopelessly in love, if her life had taken a
different course years earlier?

"Several years ago, before my father got ill, before
Max and the trial and all, my father had a couple
of poor crops—not enough rain, and an unhealthy
economy—which is always hard on farmers. Anyway,
the long and the short of it is that my father was close
to bankruptcy and needed enough money to tide him
over until he got a good crop and the economy picked
up. Not an enormous amount of money, but a large
enough sum that we had to take out a mortgage on
the island for a while. He . . . we usually kept the

island unencumbered, with only the yearly taxes and the maintenance to pay for, but we felt it was an emergency, and we were sure that things would right themselves and that we could repay the loan in no time."

"What happened?"

She shrugged, thinking her answer was obvious. "My family is lucky at love, not gambling." She sighed. So far, she hadn't been particularly lucky with either. "We had a couple more bad years with the orchard, which we'd sort of expected, but then things sort of fell apart. I went to prison, my father became ill, we kept losing money, then my father died. . . ." She lifted her head and watched a cargo ship pass by the opening of the cove. "I was in so much financial trouble by the time I was released from prison that I wanted to turn around and go back inside. I had nothing."

Payton was familiar with the word destitute, he knew what it meant, but it was something that he couldn't fully comprehend until he had experienced it. And he'd never come anywhere close.

"I used my father's life insurance money to pay off his personal debts and to pacify the banks until I could sell the orchard, and then I was going to use that money to save the island. All I needed was a little time."

Time. In his mind, there was a lot to be said for time. Time is money. Time is of the essence. Time and tide wait for no man. Time heals all wounds. Time flies. There is a time for every purpose under heaven. Frankly, he felt that now was the time—for her to sell and for him to buy.

In fact, if he were inclined to do her a favor—which he wasn't, because it wasn't his way, especially in business—he would still have to advise her to sell. Sentimental investments weren't something they taught in college or recommended in the business community. Risking what financial security she might gain from the sale of her father's apple orchard on a property that wouldn't yield a standard yearly profit for her was . . . Well, he hated to say stupid because he understood her emotional attachments, but it definitely wasn't good business. And good business was what he did. It was his life.

He sighed and turned his head to look at her. He knew what she was thinking, what she was hoping for; that he'd agree to give her the time she needed to save her island. The screwy curls around her face bounced in the wind, and he was tempted to do whatever she asked of him.

"What?" she asked, looking up to catch him staring at her with a warm, hungry light in his eyes.

"I was just wondering if you were familiar with the articles of the Geneva convention," he said. "Prisoners are to be fed at regular intervals, you know."

"Stop that. You're not my prisoner," she said, laughing as she stood and brushed the bottom of her blue jeans clean. "I thought we agreed on costrandees."

"We did," he said, following her over the rocks. "Except at mealtime. Then I'm your prisoner and you have to feed me."

The corners of her mouth turned up involuntarily. "Did I miss something? Or are you making up the rules as we go?"

"I'm making them up as we go."

"Oh. Then I think you should remain my prisoner until after the dishes are done."

"Hold it," he said, holding up a hand. "Who said you could make up rules too?"

"As costrandee, I think I have as much authority

to make up rules as you do. I also think I should get equal time at being your prisoner."

He looked shocked, but only for the second it took his hands to snake out and seize her waist. He pulled her close, and his expression changed dramatically.

"Harri, you can be my prisoner anytime you want to be. I thought I'd made that perfectly clear before now, but in case you have any doubt . . ."

He kissed her.

Somewhere in the back of her mind she was sure that there was a double standard attached to his amendments to the Geneva convention, but somehow it didn't seem to matter.

Nine

Thanksgiving came with a tail wind. It whistled through the trees and rattled the windows. It stirred angry whitecaps on the river and pushed dark clouds, heavy with rain, across the sky.

Inside the old Victorian house on Jovette Island, however, Thanksgiving was a warm, quiet olfactory orgy.

In her planning, Harriet had considered the possibility that Payton might still be quite angry with her after three days of captivity, and had thought to appeal to his stomach as a last resort in making a truce with him. She'd stocked a small turkey for the holiday, with all the trimmings, including her great-grandmother's recipe for mincemeat pie— guaranteed to please.

As it turned out, she pushed the pale, plucked poultry into the oven with a pure heart and a peaceful mind. She hummed happily over the sweet potatoes and smiled while she squished her fingers through the stuffing.

It had been several years since she'd looked forward to a holiday; several years since she'd had anything to be grateful for. This Thanksgiving was different. She was free, employed, healthy, and in love. What more could she ask for?

"Payton?" she called, entering the library where she'd expected to find him lounging in front of the fire with a thick book. "You can set the table now. Payton?"

He wasn't in the library.

She went into the dining room. The table was set, but he was nowhere in sight.

"Payton?" she called again from the foyer, raising her voice to the next floor.

"Up here." His voice was muffled as if coming from miles away.

"Where?" she called out, when he wasn't in his room either.

"Up here."

The door to the stairwell leading to the third floor stood ajar. She poked her head in and peered up at the dim light at the top of the steps.

"Up here?"

"Come on up," he said, sounding somewhat closer. "Come see what I found."

She climbed the stairs, but he wasn't on the third floor either!

"Where the hell are you?" she called, laughing. She hadn't played hide-and-seek since her childhood.

"Up here," he said again.

"Oh no. Oh, not the attic. Payton, it's filthy up there," she said, standing at the bottom of a short set of steps. She could see the gloom, smell the decades of dust and neglect, feel the cold draft, taste the mustiness—and she could hear Payton rummaging through the heaps of paraphernalia like a huge fat rat. "What are you doing up there?"

"Come and see."

"Awh," she groaned, taking the first step slowly. "Even my mother wouldn't come up here. She was a neat-nick. She asked my father to clean it once. He spent a week up here in a gas mask and said he'd only made a dent in the dust. Have you seen . . . anything?"

She heard him chuckle.

"You mean, like spiders?" he asked.

"Or bats? Anything with wings or more than two legs?"

"Nope. Not one." He looked over the banister at her. "I didn't think you'd be squeamish. I thought biologists cut up bugs and small animals for fun."

She cut him a dull glare. "Someone has to kill 'em first."

He laughed. "Who pithed your frog for you in high school?"

"Tommy Sanderson," she said, looking startled. "How did you know I couldn't do it?"

"A wild guess," he said with a casual flip of his hand. He'd spent the past four days watching her watch nature with a joy and wonderment most people saved for great sex. She was, without a doubt, the kindest, gentlest, most tenderhearted woman he'd ever met, but he wasn't sure if he could put his observations into words.

"Ah, look at you," she said, joining him in the attic. "You're a mess. What are you doing? There's stuff in your hair."

"I'm getting to know your ancestors," he said, reaching up to brush cobwebs off the top of his head. "Most of them were very snappy dressers."

"There are photo albums and portraits that could have given you a clearer picture of what they looked like," she said, frowning as she stepped over to one of several open trunks to squint and wrinkle her nose at the contents.

"This is better," he said, clearly excited and very busy at something on the far side of another open steamer trunk. "Whoever packed all this stuff did a good job. It's mostly surface dirt. The things inside these trunks are still in great shape. Of course, they reek of camphor, but old stuff does. I like it."

Now she was frowning at him.

"What are you up to?" she asked, walking toward him.

"Wait there a second, Harriet. I've hit pay dirt," he said, the enthusiasm in his voice creeping into her bones. "I found one that was the right color in one of the other trunks, but it looked a little small. This one, I think, will be perfect on you."

"On me?" She grimaced.

She watched as he held up a red satin dress, sparkling with sequins and bangles. She looked at him.

"You want me to dress up like a flapper for Thanksgiving?" she asked, mystified.

"I thought since you were going to all the trouble of a big traditional meal, that the least I could do was dress for the occasion," he said, feeling singularly silly and reckless, enjoying the mood. The last time he'd felt so young was . . . never. He'd never felt so uninhibited or carefree. "You forgot to include a tux in the clothes you bought me, and it occurred to me that there might be something up here that would do just as well."

"That was very thoughtful of you," she said, appreciating his intent. "But wouldn't you rather wear old baggy clothes, so we can pig out in comfort?"

"Sure, but this'll be more fun," he said. "Look at this." He shook the dress at her temptingly. "You're dying to try this on, right?"

Actually, she wasn't. The dress was quite beautiful and elegant, cut low in the front and back with capped sleeves and a tapered skirt that flared at the bottom. It wasn't at all her style, and she was certain she wouldn't do it justice.

But when he held up a glittering red headband with its tattered red feather still intact, grinned at her, and looked so boyishly happy, she was hard put to refuse him.

"All right," she said, conceding good-naturedly. "But don't you dare laugh at me. What are you going to wear?"

He draped the dress over her arm and handed her the headband. He considered her for a moment. His voice was soft and seductive when he said, "Red suits you."

Red—hot, bold, sensuous—she didn't think so.

"Is this what you're wearing?" she asked. He was staring at her, and it made her uncomfortable. She glanced at a black silk top hat and a pile of black material under it, hoping to divert his attention.

"All that black hair and those eyes . . ." His gaze roved over her as if he hadn't heard her. Her heart stuttered. Anticipation fluttered in her midsection. She shivered, but she wasn't cold.

"Ah, the dinner. It'll be ready in about an hour or so," she said, her throat feeling tight. "I guess if we're going to do this, we should get to it. I mean, the turkey . . . well, it'll dry out if we let it cook too long."

He loved her flustered. She always seemed to know where she was and what she was doing, except when she was flustered. Then she was shy and lost, uncertain and vulnerable. He loved her flustered.

He let the back of his knuckles drift down her soft, pale cheek. Her pupils dilated, and he felt the familiar lurch in his abdomen.

Once, he'd overheard one associate tell another that whatever Payton Dunsmore wanted, Payton Dunsmore got. It had pleased him at the time. It filled him with confidence now.

His hand turned and curved around the base of her neck as he bent his face to hers and took what he wanted. He kissed her until she staggered. He steadied her at the shoulders and then kissed her again until she moaned, and he was satisfied.

"I'll meet you downstairs in an hour," he murmured against her lips. Then as it occurred to him, he asked, "Can I help with dinner? I'm getting very good at toast."

"No," she said, backing away from him on unsteady legs. "It's all under control. I . . . it'll be ready whenever we are."

An hour later, the dinner was ready, but Harriet wasn't at all sure she was.

As she stood in the kitchen, the dazzling red dress clung loosely to the curves of her body. The flirty flounce ended just above her knees, and it didn't look too bad, in her opinion. But the scooped neck and cutout back, although modest enough, left her feeling a tad overexposed. In her self-conscious and naturally reserved mind, she had considered wearing a sweater, but something deep inside screamed, "Prude! Prude! Prude!" and she had left the sweater on her bed.

There was a knock at the kitchen door.

"I know I'm early," Payton called through the door. "But I can't stand being alone any longer. You have to see this. I look incredible."

She laughed, forgetting her meekness in the face of his arrogance. "That's a biased opinion. Come in and let me see for myself."

It was impossible to keep a straight face as he whirled into the room in black slacks and tails, long black cape flowing, top hat coming and going at the bend of his arm. He brandished a black, silver-tipped walking stick and smoothed his red cummerbund across his flat abdomen before he struck a pose, waiting for her to agree with his belief that he did indeed look incredible.

But then he looked at her—really looked at her—and before her eyes his facade crumbled. His arms lowered to his sides, his feet came together, and the air of the strutting peacock drifted away as his gaze wandered the length of her in awe.

"You're beautiful," he uttered, as if it were the first time he'd noticed.

"Thank you," she said with a reticent smile, feeling as red as her dress. "You look wonder . . . incredible, except . . ." She started to giggle.

"Except what? What are you laughing at?" he asked, pretending to be hurt. He gave himself a quick inspection and seeing that his original verdict was correct, resumed his stance.

"Your clothes are several years older than mine."

"So you like old-fashioned men," he told her. Lord help him, he wasn't feeling old-fashioned. Sequins sparkled like beckoning starlight across the curves and plains of her body. The red of the dress was bold and daring next to the pale, creamy softness of her skin. Her hair was piled intricately on the top of her head; curls dangling about her face and neck; the red headband, minus the tattered feather, woven through the dark strands. It took very little effort to imagine his fingers removing the pins or to see the mass of black hair spread out across the pillows on his bed.

"I mean, decades older."

"You prefer old, old-fashioned men."

"They're from an entirely different era, Payton," she said, laughing harder. She motioned to her own attire. "If you were the person those clothes belonged to, you wouldn't be caught dead with me. Actually, you would have been dead by the time I came along, but if you'd lived long enough, I'd be far too liberated for you. You'd have called me a . . . a . . . tart."

"A tart?" He rather liked the idea of her being a tart, but he could see that she had her heart set on looking liberated. He frowned in concentration, then came up grinning. "It's okay. We can be from different centuries if we want, because this is a magic island and I'm a magical kinda guy." He waved his silk top hat through the air twice and then glanced inside. He looked back at her, wagging his brows, enticing her to believe his fantasy.

"You pulled me out of your hat?"

"We could say that. We could say I was looking to have a tart for dessert and got you instead." He saw her chest swelling with indignation and quickly altered his story. "Or we could say that we met on a time machine that travels time like a city bus, with people getting on and off whenever they wanted to."

"Oh. I like that idea," she said, her eyes brighter than ever. "Wouldn't that be fun?"

Something came together inside of him like a tangible object. Something distantly familiar to him. He identified it as being rare and absolutely good in nature; sensed it was potentially dangerous, but for the most part it was innocent, gentle, and heartwarming. He detected a connection between it and Harriet's happiness, and that made it all the more special.

"Yes. It would be fun," he agreed absently, watching her, undergoing a slow recognition of the sensation he was feeling.

It was love. Long banished from his heart, almost forgotten, it was back. He wanted to reach out, embrace it, welcome it, but could easily recall the pain and utter devastation that had caused him to cast it out in the first place.

The light in his eyes made the nerves beneath her skin dance.

"What shall I call you," she asked. He wasn't the Payton Dunsmore she'd originally brought to the island. That one had been aloof and uncaring. The new one was warmer, happier, more outgoing. "How about Peter Peacock?"

"How about Simon Stud? You can just *Si* deeply when you want me."

She groaned playfully. The timer rang loudly, and she turned to pick up the pot holders. "And what about me? Who shall I be?"

"Hot Harriet."

"No. Nobody *chooses* to be a Harriet. How about Ruby Red." She opened the oven door, and turkey smells tickled her taste buds.

"Ravishing Ruby Red and everyone will call you Ravishing for short. Lord, that smells good."

"Have you ever carved a turkey before?"

"Can't say that I have," he said, filling his head with the aroma. "But studly men try everything at least once."

"Good. But the next time we get on the time machine, you bring along your chef and I'll bring a cleanup crew."

"An excellent idea, Ravishing."

*   *   *

Si—deeply—poured wine and lit candles while Ravishing brought the food to the table. They took turns toasting the past and the future, their good health, the food, and the roof over their heads, but they didn't voice their gratefulness for anything too personal. They didn't speak of the reawakening of long-suppressed emotions, the love that was growing stronger and stronger between them, or the contentment they felt in sharing something as simple as a Thanksgiving dinner with someone they cared about.

It was much safer for both of them to hide behind the pretense of being someone else.

"More wine, Ravishing?"

The dishes had been cleared away and the leftover food was packed in the refrigerator awaiting its next appearance, center stage. The time travelers had retired to the library and a roaring fire in the hearth.

"No, thank you." She sighed—deeply. "I still have some."

The sun had given up its efforts to shine and retired for the night, and the wind subsided enough to let the clouds slow down and dump their heavy load of rain. Drops of water pattering at the windows, the warm fire, a full tummy, and the wine were lulling Harriet to sleep.

"Can I get you anything? A pillow maybe?"

"No." Again, she sighed. "I'm perfect, just like this."

He stood and bent to kiss her sweetly.

"Yes, you are," he said softly.

Her eyes sprang open. He'd moved away to get more wine.

She listened to him pour and walk around the room. There was a small noise and a cranking sound, then he said, "I saw this the other day and wondered if it still worked."

She was about to turn around when she heard the tinkle of her great-grandfather's music box playing an old tune from the French countryside.

Payton swooped down on her in the cape he'd refused to remove even during their feast, to bow low and humbly before her.

"Miss Ravishing, will you allow me the pleasure of this dance?"

"Certainly." She sighed heavily as she got to her feet, then grinned at him. But the smile and the teasing warmth in her eyes didn't last long.

There was a fractional moment of hesitation and intense awareness between them before they moved into each other's arms. The closeness of their bodies was too real. Touching was too real. Feeling the echo to the pounding of their hearts was the most real experience they'd ever known. It showed in the tension in their muscles, the awkwardness of their hands, the slowness of their feet.

The breathing space between them might as well have been as wide and deep as a ravine, for to cross it would take bravery; would show a willingness to explore the unknown on the other side; would change the friendly equilibrium between them and alter their lives irrevocably.

Payton tried to swallow, but his throat was tight. He trembled with fear and prayed she couldn't feel it. The sun and wind scent of her filled his senses, weakening his defenses.

He was bored with the pretense. He didn't want to hold her hand and touch her lightly on the back. Nor did he want to circle the room with her, like a plastic pair of music-box dancers. He was weary with solitude and sick of the emptiness he'd imposed on himself.

Like a trickle of light into his darkness, Harriet inspired his soul to hope again. He wanted to hold her close, felt himself opening up to take her into his life. There were moments in the past few days when he would have done anything to see her slightly lopsided smile. He woke up in the morning eager to see the light in her eyes. Perhaps most astounding of all, he longed for her to like him; needed her to care about him. He wanted very much to please her and to see her happy.

Harriet was about to blow a gasket.

She was thinking of their first night together, when she'd had him nearly naked, on a bed, her hands on his smooth skin. Acute regret didn't come close to describing the bewailing of that lost moment in her heart.

She enjoyed Payton. He was easy to talk to and he made her laugh, but it wasn't enough anymore. She wanted all of him. His mind, his heart, and most immediately his body.

She ached to feel drugged by his kisses again. She craved the warmth of his body and the shivers of delight his touch induced. She released a sigh, heavy with wanting.

"What?" he said, startling her.

"I didn't say anything," she said, looking up at him. The music box was winding down, tinkling its melody slowly, softly.

"Oh. I thought you said something." His heart hammered. His legs felt shaky.

"No. I didn't."

"Were you *going* to say something?" he asked, hopeful, a throbbing beginning between his thighs.

"I don't think so." It took courage to ask someone to love you.

It had taken courage to hold her head up during the trial. It had taken courage to go to prison for a crime she hadn't committed. It had taken courage to return to face the world alone, to rebuild her life, to fight for her last chance at a happy future—the island. And it had taken more courage than she knew she had to . . . all right, kidnap him. Where the hell was all the bravery coming from? Her? Was there any left?

"You're . . . sure you weren't going to say something," he asked, watching several rapid expression changes flicker across her face.

"Well . . ." She looked over his right shoulder at nothing in particular. "I might have been going to . . . ah . . . maybe . . . ask you something."

"What?"

The music-box tinkled its last tink, while the orchestrated rhythm of the storm outside picked up its tempo, the lightning and thunder were like cymbals and drums—neither of them noticed. Their feet automatically stopped, but they remained in a dancer's embrace.

"What were you going to ask me?" Harriet at a loss for words wasn't something he'd seen before. It worried him.

"I, ah, was just going to ask if you had any questions? If there was anything you wanted to ask me or . . . ah, if there was anything else you wanted to know about me."

"Like what?"

Awh, hell. Maybe this wasn't such a great idea. Maybe all her courage was gone, used up.

"I don't know," she said, frustrated and testy. "What I've done. What I think. What I want."

"I want to know all of that," he said, beginning to recognize a certain nuance in her body language, in her eyes, in her demeanor. Excitement shot through his body and threatened to blow the top of his head off. He knew what she was asking. He knew what she wanted. All he had to do was kiss her. She would be his. It was that simple, and he could make it so easy for her. Trouble was, she was too damned cute when she was flustered! "But, off the top of my head, I can't think of anything specific."

"Oh. You feel you know me fairly well . . . then."

"I know you better than I know men and women I've worked with for ten years."

"Really?"

"Really. I've been dead inside for a long time, Harri. Pushing people away kept them from hurting me. You're the only one who's ever pushed back."

"I did?"

"In a gentle, Harrilike way you did," he said, wanting more than anything in the world to kiss the amazement from her face. "You cared, you listened, you understood. You haven't asked for or expected anything of me, but time. You've made me laugh. You've made me forget. You've led me to believe that not being perfect isn't so terrible."

"I did?"

"You did, or this island really is magic," he said. "Either way, I've fallen in love with you."

"You have? I mean, you are?"

Go for it, Harri, he prompted her from his heart. He'd backed her into a corner and was dying to see what she'd do next.

"I mean, that's good. Right?" she stammered. As a criminal, she was a nervous wreck. As a seductress she was worse. "That's . . . good. I . . . that's . . . awh, hell."

She kissed him. She wrapped her arms around his neck and pressed her lips to his so hard that there could be no mistaking what she wanted. Him.

And he let her have her way, helping where and when he could. But in the back of his mind he kept thinking that she wasn't simply another woman he wanted to have sex with. It wasn't going to be a flash in the pan or a one-night stand. He was going to make love to Harriet Wheaton, with his heart, with his soul, and with his body.

"Mmm. Harri. Slow down," he muttered against her lips, trying in vain to pull his mouth from hers. "We've got time. From now until Sunday and forever after that. Harriet?"

She couldn't hear anything but the roar of her blood in her ears. She didn't know anything but the fierce hunger that gnawed at her senses. She needed warm, soft skin and was oblivious to the popping and flying of buttons from the front of the old shirt that covered his broad, muscled chest. His bare skin at her fingertips was pure ecstasy, but she wanted nirvana. She sought to bury herself so deeply in her passion and love for him as to become insensitive to pain and reality. Her hands fumbled with his red cummerbund. She would give him bliss, but first he would explode a thousand times and cry out as he bumped into the stars.

He tried—he really•did—but it would have taken a man with superhuman strength to resist her onslaught. His resolve went up in smoke when she slipped open the fly buttons on his costume and she stroked her hands over his bare buttocks.

He felt caught in a tempest of desire that was mightier and far less manageable than the squall that raged beyond the windows. A careless flick of his wrist had the red-spangled headband sailing halfway across the room before he dug his greedy fingers into her dark tresses, dropping pins as he found them, freeing thick tumbles of soft, wavy hair. He opened his eyes long enough to satisfy himself that it was as lovely as he'd anticipated it would be, moaned with the pleasure of the feel of it, then cupped her face and obliged her with a kiss that was as eager and as ardent as her own.

Nibbling kisses on her chin and across her throat sent a heat like molten lava pouring into her breasts, filling them with an aching need of their own. She felt his hands on her thighs, working their way under her skirt, higher and higher. Warm, wet lips in the valley between her breasts released a frenzied cry from her lips. She tore at the tiny buttons securing the sparkling red dress, lowering the bodice to expose herself to his mouth.

She whimpered, and her knees buckled when his fingers found the wet fire between her legs. They staggered together until they found a solid object to support their combined weight. He pressed her back against a cool, smooth surface, his tongue tickling the roof of her mouth with delight. His hands moved around her waist, and he raised her up off the floor to suckle a throbbing nipple. She wrapped her legs around his hips and arched her back, her senses careening in a state of ecstatic triumph.

Their breath mingled in gasps, and they sobbed in a moment of supreme relief when he took her, hard and deep.

Payton was paralyzed with pleasure. She was close, hot and pulsating. He pressed her to him and held her tight, indulging his sense of achievement. His eyes opened to meet her gaze, untamed, rash, and still ravenous. Neither looked away when he thrust deeper and deeper, spiraling her toward completion.

Passion glazed her eyes, and she cried and shuddered in his arms before he took his own release. And then he lowered her slowly, until her feet touched the floor again.

Ten

Gray light filtered into the room, signaling the beginning of a new dawn. Payton's respirations were deep and regular and irrationally annoying. How could he sleep when she was still awake? Harriet wondered. On the other hand, how could she still be awake, as replete and exhausted as she felt?

She closed her dry, tired eyes and let a wave of contentment wash over her. But for her sleeplessness, she couldn't recall the last time she'd known the satisfaction and happiness that had taken up residence in her heart. She cuddled into the warmth at her back, and his arm tightened about her, possessive and protective. The limb grew lax and became heavy across her ribs as slumber pulled him back into its depths. He was far, far away, but within her reach.

A smile tugged at her lips. Payton didn't like the power she had over him, the power he'd given her. He'd get used to it, of course, but it was new and frightening to him.

"Don't do that anymore," he'd said, winded and damp with exertion.

"What?" she'd asked in much the same condition.

"Don't rush me like that." He took several deep breaths. "I want to make love to you."

"You haven't been?" She glanced at him. Flickering light from the fire in the bedroom hearth danced across his body, hid in the shadows, and shrouded them in golden intimacy.

"Slowly. I want to make love to you slowly. Drive you crazy."

"Crazier?" She groaned at the thought of it.

"I want to know every inch of you, every pore. But you get crazy and drive me crazy and . . ."

"And the rest is history?"

He chuckled. "Record-breaking history. Lord, I feel like an animal."

"A happy animal?"

"A deliriously happy animal." He rolled up on one elbow to look at her. "But I still want to taste your toes."

They wiggled in anticipation.

"Know what I think?" she asked, stretching her love-sated muscles.

"What?" he asked, watching her, resisting the urge to lick his chops.

"I don't think you're talking about the way we make love. I think you're talking about the way you lose control," she said, feeling his confusion and fear, trying to soothe him with the palm of her hand against his cheek. "Of me, certainly, which is your own fault—but you think it's even worse that you can't control yourself."

He turned his head and kissed her palm, mulling over her theory. "I've worked hard to make my life my own. It's safer if nothing means anything to me."

"I know."

"This isn't like the sex I've had with other women. I feel vulnerable to you."

"I know."

"You can manipulate me like a puppet on a string.

I go mindless with my greed to have you, to feel the way you make me feel. I'd do anything you wanted me to."

"I know." He looked as if he didn't think it possible. "I feel the same way about you. But it doesn't scare me."

"Why not?"

She shrugged her Harriet shrug. "I guess because I know you wouldn't hurt me." She reached up to caress the curls behind his ear. "You've trained yourself to attack things that are strong and threatening to you. It challenges you and keeps you safe at the same time. When we make love, you know— deep in your heart—you know I'm as defenseless as you feel. And you won't hurt anything weaker than yourself."

"How do you know?" he asked, his eyes keen and narrowed. "What makes you think that you know me so well?"

She could tell by the tension and the hint of suspicion in his voice that she was going to get only one chance to answer correctly. She held his trust in her hands by a tenuous thread.

"Remember when I told you how disillusioned I became after what happened to me? How I couldn't believe in anything anymore?"

"Yes."

"I used to ask myself, over and over, what had I done wrong? What did I miss? Why didn't I see it coming? Why didn't I do things differently? I had a lot of time to think it over, and do you know what I finally decided?"

"What?"

"That I wouldn't have done anything differently. Everything I did was right for me at the time." She could see that he didn't understand. "I made the best decisions I could with the information I had. My instincts weren't wrong, they just weren't completely informed."

His frown deepened. She rolled onto her own elbow to face him. "The job change was an incredible career opportunity. I took it. It was the right thing to do. The project was worth every second I devoted to it. It was a good thing to do, and I'd do it again in a second. Max is a genius. That's documented. He's basically a good man, and he has a track record to prove it. I saw with my own eyes his compassion, his gentleness, and his understanding, and my instincts responded appropriately—also not a bad thing. What I couldn't see, what I couldn't prove later, was that he was also an unethical coward. *He* committed the crime. Not me. *He's* the one who couldn't face the consequences of his actions. Not me."

"Yeah. And you're the one who paid the price. Not him."

"You think not?" she asked wisely. "I know Max Goldtharpe. There's a lot more good in the man than bad. I believe he's paying a much higher price than I paid for what he did."

"Your wishful thinking."

"It's not. I believe it. I also believe in me, which is how I found the courage to fight you for this island. And I believe in you, which is why I can trust you."

"But you believed in and trusted the good doctor, too, didn't you?"

"Yes."

"Then how do you know I won't chew you up and spit you out in the trash; finish the destruct-o-job he started on you."

"I don't," she said, smiling at him. "I could be making another big mistake."

"Doesn't that scare you?"

"I think it would be scarier to spend the rest of my life in the constant fear of making another mistake."

Payton didn't comment, and their drowsy voices began to speak of other things. School dances. Blind dates. Memorable firsts. However, Harriet noticed, when touches started to linger and sweet-pecking kisses lengthened to the deep, wet mind-boggling variety, Payton was more determined than ever to control his passion.

He'd held her hands above her head and drove her slowly, carefully, and quite thoroughly out of her mind; tormenting her inch by inch, until his senses exploded, shattering his precious control. He lost his battle again—and she had a feeling she was going to enjoy his war—but he accepted his defeat in a most accommodating manner, caressing and cuddling close to his new weakness until he fell asleep.

So? Why couldn't she sleep? What was nagging at her? What had she forgotten? What had she left half-finished? What was wrong?

"Well, let's see here," Payton said later that morning, rubbing his hands together over a suitcase of clothes. "Which great little outfit should I wear today? The blue polo with khaki slacks for a casual look or the white oxford with blue denim for a casual look?"

"I blew it, didn't I?" she asked from the bed where she was tying her shoes, though her gaze was fixed on a magnificent specimen of the human male wrapped in a bath towel. "You're that one in a million man who likes to wear a tie all the time, aren't you?"

"As a matter of fact, I hate ties. I grew up in a tie. I forget to wear one every chance I get."

"Oh. Good."

Something in her voice made him turn toward her. She looked pale and tired and . . . sort of solitary. So he sat down beside her.

"I guess I should be glad that you don't have a tolerance for late-night cavorting," he said, gently tracing the dark shadows beneath her eyes. "But I feel like a heel for doing this to you. I shouldn't have been so greedy."

"I like you greedy." She emphasized the period on her sentence with a stingy kiss. "But if you don't put on something other than that towel pretty soon, I'll have to show you what greedy really is."

"Okay." He kissed her back, and for a second or two she wasn't sure if his answer meant okay, I'll get dressed, or okay, show me what greedy really is.

He cupped her face in his hands and studied it closely.

"Are you all right?"

"Yes. I'm fine."

"Worried about anything? Want to talk?"

His concern was heartwarming, and she smiled. "I'm fine."

"Just fine?"

"Happy. Content. Delirious. Amazed."

"Scared? Nervous?"

"That too."

"Wondering about the future?"

"A little."

"Want to talk about the island?"

"No," she said quickly and emphatically, a sudden panic rising up within her. It was as if he'd stuck a pin in the tissue surrounding an open wound, not quite touching the source of the pain, but hitting too close to it. "I don't want to talk business until we get back to St. Peter's Bay on Sunday. Okay?"

"Why not?"

"Please. Whatever you decide to do, don't tell me until after we leave the island."

He considered her request, then nodded. "Okay. But in the meantime, you have to promise not to worry about my decision. Your eyes are sad and troubled. They're tearing me apart. I want to make the rest of your life as smooth as glass. No troubles. No worries. No pain. I want to make you happy. I want to see it in your eyes."

He did make her happy, and she let him see it.

"So this is where it all started," he said, ducking his head low to enter the crude log cabin on the northeastern side of the island.

"No. This is phony. It was built in thirty-six or thirty-eight, in there as a sort of shrine or something to the past. The only thing original here is the stone fireplace. That's how they knew there was a cabin here once. Though it wasn't Lazare's—the fireplace is too well made. His would have been more primitive, simpler."

"So whose estate was this?"

"Lazare's grandchildren and their children lived here, and maybe one more generation after that. Then the family moved to higher land and built where the house is now, but that house was torn down when they decided to build the Victorian. There are sketches of it somewhere, I think."

He chuckled, running a hand over the smooth round stones of the ancient fireplace. "You know, for the last of the line of Jovettes, you're not exactly exacting with your information." He tried to mimic her. "It was my great-grandfather or maybe his son or was it his father. . . ."

"Listen," she said, taking no offense. "I'm doing the best I can. Have you got any idea how many historians there've been in this family? Have you got any idea how many *stories* there are to tell? And, unfortunately, I spent a lot of time trying not to listen to all the old stories my grandparents and my mother used to tell." She paused, thoughtful. "If you're really interested, it's all written down somewhere. The library's my guess."

"Your guess?" His expression was dubious. "You know exactly where it's all written down. This place may not have meant anything to you when you were young, but it means everything to you now."

Everything? No, not everything, she thought, watching Payton look out one of the tiny windows toward the north shore. The island and its history meant something to her, had meant a lot to her a week ago, but everything? No. Payton was everything.

The revelation stuck in her throat, hard. Payton was everything. Compared to him, the island was a picayune lump of rock. Compared to losing Payton, losing the island was like losing air when you exhaled.

"Harriet." Her gaze met his. He'd been watching her. "What are you thinking?"

"That the past isn't important. That what really counts is the present."

"That's very deep," he said, trying to tease the frown from her brow, feeling troubled because she was. "Come here." She slipped between his arms, and he leaned back against the wall for support. "Are you thinking that your past might make a difference to me, that I care whether or not you've been to prison?"

"Well, no, I hadn't thought about it. Does it?"

"No. Other than the fact that I want to break that damned doctor's neck for you."

"What if I were guilty?" she asked, curious. "Would it matter then?"

"I don't know," he said, wanting to be truthful. "One of the things I love about you is your honesty. Being a crook would kind of rescind that, wouldn't it?"

"So you believe I'm innocent."

"No. I think you're a lot of things, but innocent isn't one of them. But . . . *but*," he repeated when she gasped. "I know you don't lie and you don't steal."

"Why don't you think I'm innocent?" she asked, half-offended.

"You cheat at pool," he said. She sputtered. His heart chuckled, and he anticipated the fun of ruffling her feathers again. Lord, he loved her flustered. "You're a kidnapper. You kiss like a hooker. And—"

"A hooker!"

"A high-priced hooker. One worth kissing."

"A hooker?"

"One who knows how to make a kiss something a man could die for."

"They kiss that well?"

"No. But you do," he said, lowering his mouth to hers.

"Know what I want to do?"

"Oh, not the cape and top hat again?" She groaned, her head falling to his chest. "No more swooping through the halls, no more blood sucking."

"You loved it."

"I did. But no more tonight. I'll have nightmares."

"Okay, but that's not what I wanted to do anyway."

"What then?"

"Let's watch those old movies of when you were a kid."

"No."

"I'll start a fire in the library and you can make popcorn, and we'll watch baby Harriet grow up."

"Absolutely not."

"Why? I want to see what you looked like then."

"I was ugly and there's all sorts of naked baby butt shots and toothless smiles and falling off bikes and skates. They aren't flattering films."

"I've already seen your fine naked butt. And falling off bikes and losing your teeth is all kid stuff. There are movies of me doing the same things," he said. Then as if to entice her further, he added, "I'll show you mine, if you'll show me yours."

She giggled. And then she felt it.

"Uh-oh. It's starting. We're almost out." She shuffled and turned to let the tepid water shower down on Payton's shoulders. "If we don't get out soon, we'll be frozen like this forever."

"Okay." His kiss was long and lingering, and the water grew cooler.

"Okay, we'll get out?" she asked, laughing, throwing off her first shiver against the cold. "Or okay, we'll be frozen like this forever?"

"Yes," he said, reaching behind him to cut off the shower. "I wouldn't mind being like this with you forever." He placed a wet kiss on her wet nose. "But yes, we'd better get out."

He reached for her towel first, wrapping her tightly and rubbing hard to warm her. Then he brushed the water from his hair with his own towel and, tucking it around his waist, left the steamy bathroom. "Don't go anywhere," he said.

She was dry and had released her long braid from its pins by the time he returned.

"Here," he said, tossing her the top half of the obscene Mickey and Minnie pajamas, the bottoms already tied snugly about his narrow hips. "A mind is too great a thing to waste, and whoever dreamed these things up was a genius—or a pervert. Let's see how many of these positions are really possible. We'll cross them off one by one."

"Are you kidding?" she asked, examining the illustrations with a furrowed brow. "There's no two alike. It'll take us a month to try them all. . . . not to mention the months of physical therapy afterward."

"Oh, I don't know," he said, stepping close to her, sliding his hands down her soft, smooth curves. "Your agility has amazed me a couple times already."

"Stop that," she murmured, her mind fuzzy with sensation, her skin flushed—not from the shower.

The now familiar clutching in his abdomen triggered his unprecedented and perpetual hunger for the slim, slightly imperfect woman he held. Her immediate response to his touch fed his urge to exert control over her. The haze of passion in her eyes made him feel powerful. The thrill of feeling her tremble in his arms lent him an air of omnipotence.

He smiled and helped her into the pajama top. The sensations he felt were precious, but fleeting and false. Her power over him was far greater, deeper, and infinitely more satisfying to him. He was like an ill-fated pyromaniac—driven, compelled to light the fires, only to find himself caught, trapped, and doomed to perish in the flames.

He couldn't think of a better way to die.

"Still cold?" he asked, buttoning only the three middle buttons, deliberately skimming his knuckles against her pelvic region.

Hardly, she thought.

"Freezing. I think I'll get a robe," she said, stepping around him to the door. "Better yet, I have flannel pajamas with feet in them."

"With? Wait a second," he said, confused, following her out into the hall and into his bedroom. "Get into bed. I'll keep you warm."

"I'm chilled to the bone," she said, stalling for time, heading for the hidden hallway between their rooms. "I'll get my coat too."

"Come back here. I'll take the chill out of your bones."

With door handle in hand she turned to him, vibrant, vivacious, the vision of a vamp.

"You'd do that?" she asked, playing sweet and seductive, fully aware of the slit openings of the pajama top. "You'd warm up my bones for me?"

Quick to catch on and fast to rise to the occasion, Payton inched forward. "Come here and see."

"Uh-uh." She shook her head. "You want these bones, you've got to catch them."

He was on to her before she finished her sentence. She slammed the door in his face and raced to the other end of the hall, locking that door behind her. By the time he reached it, and swore a blue streak on the other side, she was leaving her room by the other door.

Excitement made her giggle as she bound from the last step on the main floor, just as Payton began his descent. His great long legs were his advantage, but she was agile and she knew the house better. There were several close calls but she managed to elude him, until she crept into the long unused ballroom and pressed herself against the wall to catch her breath.

The air was musty and chilled. The floor was ice-cold, and it stung her toes. But even before she could breathe regularly again, she was mesmerized by the beauty of the moon glowing through the walls of glass, spreading a gossamer carpet of silver across the floor.

The room was enchanted with the sparkle of frost on the windows. Friendly shadows beckoned her, invited her to the party.

She stepped away from the wall and was suddenly bathed in pixie light; her arms and legs were pale, graceful, luminous. As if by magic, he emerged from the darkness, tall and silent.

"So beautiful," she said, her voice hardly more than a breath of air.

"So beautiful," he agreed, his gaze fixed on the vision of her.

They paced to the middle of the huge room and wordlessly embraced. They danced, circling, round and round. Neither was cold, neither was too sure they were even awake.

"It is like magic, isn't it?" he said, his voice a reverent whisper, as if he were dancing in a holy place.

Magic.

Magic.

The word pierced her heart and mind in one swift, brutal thrust. It was magic. She was screaming and sick inside. It was magic. She stumbled, and he wrapped his arms about her.

"I'm cold," she murmured around the painful lump in her throat. It was magic.

"Let's go upstairs." His lips pressed against her temple as he turned them to the wide oaken doors. His heart was brimming with love and protectiveness and . . . it was magic.

"Love me, Payton. Hold me."

"I do. I am. I will."

She had to tell him. It was magic. She had to tell him. But she wanted just one more night.

"All night. Till morning."

"All night." He kissed her as they mounted the stairs. "And all day tomorrow. And all day the day after, and the day after that."

She pressed closer and heard the steady rhythm of his life.

It was magic.

It was simply magic.

Only magic.

Eleven

Men always took bad news better with a full stomach—didn't they?

Harriet wasn't sure if anything was going to make what she had to tell Payton any easier, but cooking their breakfast kept her from biting her nails to nubs and held her tears at bay.

At least she'd finally realized why she wasn't sleeping well. How could she have been so stupid? So thoughtless? So cruel? How could she possibly sleep ever again, unless her conscience was clear?

She closed her eyes and ground her teeth. She would have the rest of her life to call herself names and flog herself.

Payton was the true victim, and she had to tell him.

"Have you seen the snow?" he asked, coming into the kitchen behind her, his hair still damp from his shower.

She glanced out the window. Snow was beginning to stick to the grass and trees, the beginnings of a winter wonderland—she couldn't have cared less. Spring could have been in full bloom and the world would have looked just as bleak to her.

"Think we'll be lucky and get snowed in here before tomorrow?" he asked, sounding far too chipper on such a rotten morning.

"No."

His brows rose perceptively. She was slow to wake in the mornings, but she usually wasn't grouchy.

He circled the work island and turned her to face him. There were dark shadows beneath her eyes again.

"I'm sorry," he said, distressed. "I did it again, didn't I?"

"What?"

"Kept you up too late. I tried—"

"No. I'm not tired," she said, brusque in her dread. "Here. Eat. We need to talk."

He took the plate from her, his confusion plain on his face.

"Okay. Let's talk."

"Eat first."

"I see. We're going to *talk*, not have breakfast conversation," he said, following her to the table. "Must be serious."

"Eat." She was afraid she'd lose her nerve, take a coward's way out.

The meal passed in silence, the tension between them escalating until Payton popped the last bite of toast into his mouth, finished his coffee, and cleared away his dishes. He sat opposite her, laced his fingers together, and ordered her to speak.

"Let's have it," he said, a successful businessman who was used to getting to the point and facing problems head-on.

Her heart felt as hard and cold as ice, and it hurt as if it had been dropped and cracked in a thousand places.

"Payton, I don't know how to tell you this without . . ." *Hurting you,* she was about to say. The thought was impossible to voice aloud.

"I've made a terrible mistake, Payton, and I . . ." want to say I'm sorry, she thought. Sorry wasn't enough. "What I've done is unforgivable."

"Come on, Harri," he said, half-amused with her inability to complete a sentence. "You've spied on me, interfered with my business, and kidnapped me. How bad could it be?"

"Bad. I . . ."

His brows rose higher to indicate his interest as he patiently waited for her to finish. There was no good or easy way to tell him, she finally decided, chewing her lower lip. She took a deep breath. "I let myself fall in love with you."

"Well," he said, taken back. He wanted to laugh but sensed danger in the undercurrent of her words. "That *is* unforgivable."

"I promised you I wouldn't, remember?"

"No."

"I forced you to come here and to fall in love with me," she said, words beginning to roll like an avalanche from her mouth. "I brought you to the island specifically to expose you to the magic, to show you it was real, so you could understand the importance of my keeping the island. I . . . I thought I could handle it, that I'd keep my head on straight. I didn't think I'd fall in love with you too. I thought I might learn to like you eventually, which would be proof enough for me that the magic worked. But then . . . I didn't mean to fall in love with you, and I certainly didn't mean for you to love me. I thought you might end up liking me a little, but I had no idea how powerful the magic really was."

"Harri," he said, touching her hand, trying to calm her and his heart at the same time. "You don't really think I love you because I've fallen under some sort of spell or something, do you?"

"Don't you? Aren't you convinced yet?"

"I'm convinced that I love you, but the only spell I've fallen under is yours. It doesn't have anything to do with the island, and it certainly isn't magic."

"How do you know?"

"Because I know, dammit," he said, fear creeping like a fungus inside him.

"You can't know. And it would be so unfair of me to take advantage of you under these circumstances. So, tomorrow—"

"Tomorrow, I'm still going to love you."

"Perhaps. But when the boat takes us back to St. Peter's Bay tomorrow, I'll be going straight to the sheriff's office to confess everything I've done to you, and you'll go back to your life. That was the deal."

"The deal?" he said, his eyes narrowed, his fear turning to excruciating pain. "The deal? Is that all this was to you?"

"That's not how it turned out, no. But it was a deal. I promised you that I wouldn't hold you to anything when it was over. I shouldn't have let it go so far. I can't regret it for myself, but I do for you."

"This is crazy," he said, as if to alert her to the world's sudden madness. "It's crazier than you kidnapping me in the first place."

Who knew better than she?

"I . . . I said I'd let you decide what to do with the island once we determined whether or not the magic was real. So, I'll—"

"Real?" He stood with enough force to push his chair over. "I'll tell you what's real. I'm real. You're real. And what we feel is real."

"You're right," she said, reaching to touch him, needing to touch him, to ease his pain, to soothe him. He pulled his hand away. "But don't you see, that's the trouble with magic. It all seems so real, but it's not. I tricked you. It's not love we feel, it's just the magic."

"To hell with the magic," he bellowed, wanting to scream like a lunatic. "There is no magic. There never was. I can't explain what happened to all your damned ancestors or how all this nonsense got started, but there's no such thing as magic or love potions or anything else. If anything, we made our own magic."

"I know this must be difficult for you to understand. And I don't like it any more than you do," she said, the cracks in her heart beginning to bleed. "But I could never live with you, or myself, knowing that I'd tricked you, forced you to love me."

"You didn't," he stated, then suddenly decided to change tracks. "You're right. You did trick me. You forced me to fall in love with you, and I demand that you accept responsibility for your actions. I insist that you stay with me until I fall out of love with you."

She stood before him with a bittersweet smile for his cleverness.

"I wish . . ." it were real, she wanted to say. But it felt too real to make it sound otherwise.

"What? You wish what?"

"I wish you great happiness, Payton. I wish you knew how much you deserve to be happy. And I hope . . ." her voice faltered, "I hope you'll let some other woman see what you've shown me. That you're good and kind and loving."

He saw the tears in her eyes and wanted to shake her.

"Harriet, stop this. I don't want another woman. I want you."

"Why?"

"Why? Because I love you!"

"Why do you love me?"

"Because . . ." He was a fast thinker, he could do this. "Because . . ." There were a thousand reasons globbed together into one huge unexplainable emotion. "Because I do."

"You see," she said gently. "It's just the magic."

Payton wanted to tear his hair out; he wanted to tear *her* hair out. By late afternoon he was desperate to do something to get her attention.

She'd spent the day gathering her personal possessions—things that didn't belong to the house— and packing them into boxes.

"I'll arrange to have these removed from the house as soon as possible. They'll need to go into storage with the rest of my things," she told him in passing, stepping around him as he tried to impede her progress.

"Storage? Why do you have things in storage?"

"They aren't yet," she said casually, labeling the contents of a half-filled box. "But they don't let you take a lot of personal stuff to prison, you know."

"For crissake! Will you stop? You aren't going to prison. You know I won't press charges."

"Yes, and I've been giving that some thought," she said, calm and serious when she looked at him. "It is possible that it may take some time, several days, a week or more maybe for the magic to wear off, and you'll feel more inclined to press charges then. I just wanted to mention to you that if the authorities can't locate me here or in St. Peter's Bay, that the only other place I plan to go is back to Massena. They can contact me through the college, or I can write down my address for you, if you'd like."

He left the room, swearing and muttering unintelligibly, too dumbfounded to argue.

He gave her plenty of time to reconsider between his next two attempts to make her see reason, not that it did any good. He entertained the notion of dropping something on her head to pound some sense into her, but decided that with his luck she'd develop amnesia and forget who he was altogether. During dinner he was tempted to choke her until she agreed to be logical, but the mere thought of his hands on her throat brought the customary clutching sensation to his abdomen. When she bid him good night at *her* bedroom door, it was all he could do to keep from dragging her to the floor and using all he'd discovered about her body to bring her mind to order. But he was all too conscious of who controlled whom in the throes of passion and thought it safer not to— for fear she'd convince him to have her sent to the electric chair before they were finished.

It wasn't until after he'd spent several hours tossing in bed, his muscles aching with tension, his mind weary with worry, that his fear and frustration took on the colors of anger and pain.

Past and present merged, festered, and poisoned his perspective on the future.

Effortlessly, he donned the old cloak of indifference that he called pride. He was not a man to make compromises in his life; he didn't beg, and he wouldn't be controlled. He didn't feel pain, and he couldn't be broken. Possessions were of little consequence to him—people even less.

By morning meaningful dialogue was no longer an option. Harriet suffered quietly, stoically, seemingly calm and resigned to her fate. Payton agonized safe inside his shell, coolly superior, indifferent, sarcastic. Conversation remained at a one word minimum—two maximum.

"Coffee?"

"Thanks."

"Eggs?"

"No."

"Stopped snowing."

"Swell."

"More toast?"

"No."

"Finished?"

"Need help?"

"No. Thanks."

"Boat's here."

"Swell."

"Hi, Tony."

"Tony Saone. Payton Dunsmore."

"Hello."

"You okay?"

"Yes."

One of them turned lime-green on the way back to St. Peter's Bay, but managed to retain his dignity—as well as his breakfast toast. The other, wisely, maintained a strict silence until they were soundly on shore.

"Your room is still available at the inn," she said, standing beside him after Tony Saone, their rescuer, dropped them at the end of the dock and proceeded on to the marina. "The limousine will be back at one o'clock to take you wherever you want to go."

"Fine." Just to prove to himself that he could, he walked away from her—but he felt no satisfaction.

"Payton?" she called after him. He stopped but didn't turn. "I'm . . . sorry."

"I'm sure you are."

"Payton?" she called again, stopping him once more. "I won't forget you. Ever."

He turned to her then. Sad brown eyes met frozen emerald-green ones. His voice was equally cold but soft when he finally replied, "Ever is a long time, Harri."

Twelve

Payton Dunsmore had wasted no time foreclosing on Harriet's island. The mortgage and back taxes owed on Jovette Island were paid in full before the end of November, and the title changed hands via the attorneys and realtors. She neither saw nor heard from Payton during the transaction, though she waited daily for the police to appear on her doorstep.

Christmas was a dismal affair. The campus was deserted, and the town of Massena burrowed itself in against the cold, for a holiday season of quiet *family* gatherings. Overnight, it became a new year. To celebrate, Harriet hung up a new calendar. Classes resumed, the winter term was well under way, and still there was no dulling of the ache she carried in her heart, no release from the longing in her spirit, no dwindling of the love she felt for the man she'd left in St. Peter's Bay nearly three months earlier. The magic wasn't wearing off as she had thought it would, as she had prayed it would with time.

She sincerely hoped that Payton wasn't suffering in the same state of suspended animation; that the force that had linked them so closely on the island had dispelled itself, left him free to resume his life without her.

She hoped it, truly and with almost every fiber of her being—almost. For deep inside, so deep and so well buried in guilt that her conscious mind couldn't acknowledge it; so deep that only her dreams could attest to the fact, she was watching for him, waiting for him, sure that he would come for her.

"Bundle up before you go out this morning," the radio announcer warned her. "It's biting cold—excellent hog-killin' weather for those of you who've got'em."

Harriet turned off the radio; the daily farm report was her cue to leave the house within three minutes or be late for her first morning class. Why she knocked herself out getting to school on time, when most of her students didn't wake up until *after* class anyway, was beyond her. She suspected it had something to do with responsibility and setting a good example and getting paid a regular salary, but an eight A.M. biology lab was too much, even for her. Next year she'd schedule differently.

If there was a next year, she thought, locking her front door on the way out. She was always a bit surprised to walk out of her house and not find it surrounded by police cars, lights flashing, the officers armed and alert. How long was it going to take for the magic to wear off? How long before Payton came to his senses and took his revenge? She wouldn't consider the possibility that he'd exact his vengeance by doing nothing at all to her. He wasn't a cruel man, just slow to recover.

The car keys slipped from her gloved hand. She fumbled blindly for them on the floorboard, her mind quickly reviewing the morning lesson plan.

The used compact car she'd acquired to replace the pride and joy she'd driven three years earlier, when she could afford frequent timing adjustments and tune-ups from expensive foreign car dealerships, was nothing if not dependable. The engine turned over with the first twist of the ignition, though she could tell from its sputtering that it wasn't eager to be disturbed so early and on such a chilly morning.

Music filled the car.

She glanced at the radio. It wasn't on.

It was a mellifluous tinkling, like a music box. The tune was familiar, but she couldn't name it. She turned the engine off, and the car went silent. She turned the key in the ignition again, and the melody started once more. She opened the car door, then quickly closed it. The music was playing outside the car as well as inside. She turned the engine off and got out.

Harriet was no mechanic, still nothing under the hood appeared to have been tampered with.

With her hands on her hips, the only logical explanation she could come up with was that she was the victim of a practical joke. It hadn't been so long ago that she couldn't remember her own college days. Higher education hadn't evolved much in those years, and its students were still half-adult, half-child creatures who needed an outlet, she thought, trying not to be too angry.

She looked at her watch. She was going to be late. The questions now were, was she going to miss class completely while she tore her car apart looking for the source of the music; was she going to miss half the class walking to school or was she going to be a little tardy by driving to the science building in what now sounded like an ice-cream truck?

Why me? she wondered, driving down Main Street, ignoring the curious glances, grateful that it was too early for the entire town of Massena to be out and about. Didn't she have enough on her mind? Was she such an awful teacher? Was this retaliation for an eight A.M. biology lab? Or was she simply the easiest target, being the newest and the only unmarried female member of the staff?

Heads turned, fingers pointed, and students produced a riot of laughter as she drove down the lane toward her office. She pulled into her parking space and quickly put an end to the infernal noise that announced her arrival.

"Sorry. All sold out," she said, responding to various requests for ice-cream bars and pops, trying to maintain the facade of a good sport while she felt red-cheeked and undignified. "No. I'm out of cherry Popsicles too. Better luck tomorrow."

She was pleased that her class had taken the initiative to begin the lab without her, though they were all under suspicion until she discovered who the uncouth car culprit was. Biology could be a disgusting science if one put her mind to it, she decided vengefully.

This term, the lab was for junior embryologists, studying the development of animals from fertilized egg through the birth or hatching process.

"So, if heat is all a fertilized egg needs to develop and eventually hatch, why wouldn't turning up the heat a little, say a degree or two or three—why wouldn't that speed up the process?" she asked the class.

When no one answered, she looked up from the incubator she was adjusting—and that's when she saw them.

Bubbles. Thousands of free-floating bubbles pouring into her classroom through an air vent above the door at the back of the room.

"Oh, this is too much," she said, still half angry

from the last prank she'd been on the receiving end of. "I want this to stop immediately."

The bubbles ignored her. The students looked confused—and more than a little amused.

"I mean it. Whoever is responsible for this, please turn the bubbles off now."

She looked from one blank face to the next, and when she could not perceive any guilt, she marched to the back of the room and opened the door to the hall. Stepping out and looking up, she saw that the vent was one-sided, opening only into her classroom.

"What is this?" she asked herself aloud.

"Bubbles," one of her more astute pupils answered.

"I can see they're bubbles," she said, the strain on her temper quivering in her voice. "But where are the bubbles coming from?"

"That air vent," the same student said. He grinned at her, and she made a mental note to give him a failing grade.

"Get me something to plug this up with, please," she said to no one special, pulling a chair under the vent. "This isn't Friday the thirteenth or April Fool's Day. I must have missed the advent of the new world order and the institution of Get Miss Wheaton Day."

A bloodcurdling scream scurried straight up her spine, throwing her off balance, nearly toppling her from the chair.

"What on earth . . ." she said, righting herself and looking about.

The ceiling was covered with helium-filled balloons, and still they continued to rush out of the supply closet, two and three at a time. Big, bright red balloons.

The startled student who'd freed them had since recovered and was giggling in wonder and delight.

"They say 'I love you,' " she said, looking at Harriet.

"What?"

"The balloons. They have 'I love you' written on them." She grabbed one as it floated by and turned the worded side to Harriet. "See. 'I love you.' "

She could feel all the blood draining from her face and her heart beginning to race as she looked to each of the girls in the class. None of them was inclined to accept the rather overzealous declaration of love and seemed bent on thinking that the balloons belonged to her.

"But I'm not seeing anyone right now," she said, her hands held out in supplication.

She felt a draft from the door behind her as it opened, but before she could turn around, there was a flash of light and a thick cloaking puff of smoke.

She screamed and crouched low, covering her head with her arms.

"Maybe you're not seeing anyone right now because you aren't looking," she heard a familiar voice say.

She didn't move. She was going to wait until she woke up and call it all a bad dream.

"Harriet," the voice said, cool and calm. "I'm making a fool of myself for you. The least you could do is pay attention."

She groaned and relinquished her fate to destiny.

When she could bring herself to look at him, he flapped his black cloak at her, snapping it in the air.

"Payton. . . ."

"See. I knew she'd remember me," he said, addressing the class. He stepped around Harriet, grinned at a young woman with a particularly stupid look of awe on her face, and swooshed his wrap dramatically. "Is this cape great, or what?"

There was a general murmur that it was indeed a great cape, and he smiled at his audience with pleasure.

"Payton. Please," she said, picturing herself jobless and destitute. "What are you doing here?"

"I'm here to tell you that I love you."

Why wasn't she thrilled? For one, they had a lot to talk about before they could discuss love. Two, she was sure he was still suffering from the effects of the island's magic. And thirdly . . .

"This isn't the best time or place to get into this, Payton."

"I don't know," he said. "I think my timing is as good as yours was when you kidnapped me." To the chorus of gasps and grumbles from the students, he simply grinned and nodded. "It's true. I'll bet you didn't know that your little teacher here is capable of almost anything, including kidnapping, for the sake of love."

His gaze caught and held hers as he moved toward her. Passion stormed like an angry sea in the depths of his eyes. Her breath caught in her throat, and her tongue stuck to the dry roof of her mouth. She felt dizzy from the hammering of her heartbeat in her ears. He curled his arms around her waist and pulled her close—she couldn't pull away.

"She lured me into a trap. She kidnapped me," he said, his voice soft. "She seduced me and cast a magic spell over me. She made me fall in love with her." And in quite a different voice he added, "Then she broke my heart."

He moved away from her in a flaring flurry of black silk, leaving her dazed and helpless to stop him.

"Can you believe it?" he asked his fans—and no they couldn't. "Look at her." An arm and the cape pointed in her direction. "So beautiful. So sweet and innocent looking. So appealing . . . and yet, so treacherous."

That brought her back to reality.

"Treacherous? Me?" She was floored. And getting angry. "You were never in any danger. And the one time I thought you were, I was prepared to take you straight back to St. Peter's Bay and turn myself in— but as it turned out, *you* were lying to me."

"And you were always truthful with me?"

"After I sank the dinghy, yes."

"So, you really loved me?"

"Yes."

"And do you still?"

Her mouth opened and closed, but nothing came out. She wanted to say no. It was the best answer. It would hurt them both, but the spell needed to be broken, he needed to go on with his life. However, no wasn't a truthful answer. She did love him.

"Ah. She's speechless. A rare and encouraging event," he said. "Because, you see, she's usually very opinionated, and she doesn't hesitate to speak her mind."

"I'm not opinionated. I have opinions, yes, but—"

"She also thinks she's an authority on magic."

"I never said that," she protested. "And I suppose you think the stunts you pulled with my car and the bubbles were magic?"

"Nah. They were nothing. Anyone can make a car play 'This Magic Moment' and blow bubbles through an air vent." From up his sleeve he withdrew a solitary long-stemmed red rose. "Here. This is for you. A token of my love."

She wouldn't take it.

"It's real, like my love for you. I have scratches on my arm to prove it. Smell it."

He was cajoling, and she loved him so dearly, she found it hard to refuse him anything. She leaned forward slightly and took in the sweet distinctive fragrance of the rose.

The rose spit in her face.

Payton chuckled, and the class was in stitches as she wiped drops of water from her face.

"That's cute, Payton. But it isn't magic. It's a trick. And a stupid trick at that."

"I know, but watch this."

From the deep, dark recesses of his fabulous frock he produced a bottle of champagne, a crystal glass, and a white envelope. He started to open the bottle of wine as he spoke.

"Most magicians use milk and a newspaper for this trick because it's easier to see, but I like doing things my own way," he explained as he worked. And to maintain a constant banter, a trick of the trade, he said, "I'm that kind of man. I'm used to snapping my fingers and getting what I want. I'm used to having things my own way. I make sure I'm always in control." Pop! "I used to anyway. But I'm changing." He looked at Harriet. "You changed something in me. I never let anyone have so much control over me. I felt safe with you."

He poured wine into the glass and handed it to her. He took up the envelope, removed a sheet of paper, and began to fold it. "I haven't let anything or anyone mean anything to me for years, because what I didn't care about, I couldn't miss." He stopped to meet her gaze. "But I've never been in love like this. I've never felt as if I had so much to lose before."

He held the cone-shaped piece of paper out to her, and she automatically poured the wine into it, too moved and confused to speak, too much in love and in too much pain to do more than listen and watch.

He unfolded the paper, and with his back to her, he showed his audience the wine was missing. He began to refold the paper.

"But how could I argue with magic?" he asked the crowd, and then turning back to her, he said, "I didn't know how to fight for you against something that couldn't be seen or touched or heard. You're a provoking, irritating, and really frustrating woman, Harriet Wheaton. Traits, one and all, that I love about you, by the way."

He turned to her expectantly and traded her the paper for the glass.

Speaking out of the side his mouth, he instructed her to, "Shake the paper out and show them that it's as dry as a bone."

She started to unfold the paper, the process slowing when she noticed the print on it. Script print. A state seal. It was a land deed . . . to Jovette Island . . . in the name of Harriet Martha Jovette Wheaton Dunsmore.

"Oh, Payton, no," she said with a gasp, with no inkling of what to think or say or do.

He saved her the trouble of having to decide just then, by placing a silencing finger to her lips.

"You asked me why I loved you, and I told you I didn't know," he said, as if they were alone in the room. "Well, I've been busy the last few months. I have a list of reasons." He took another sheet of paper from his pocket and began to read. "Your mouth is crooked. Your eyes are brown. I love those little wispy curls around your face." His fingers moved from her mouth to touch them. "You're smart. You're funny. You look great in bubbles. You care about the world. You're forgiving. You're gentle and sweet."

"Payton. Stop."

"You're a fairly decent cook. You're patient as hell. You'd leave the lights on and your door open. You're clever and sneaky. You're brutally truthful unless you need to lie, and then you *omit* rather than tell lies. You can bore a man to the point of tears when you're talking about biology, but I love your enthusiasm on the subject. I've never known a woman who could do the things you do to me in bed."

"Payton. Enough."

"There's more. You're illogical and stubborn. You have an irrational belief in magic which is contrary to everything else you believe about life—and that's where I screwed up."

"No. You did nothing wrong. It was my fault," she said, weak and wishing he'd hold her. But he went on as if he hadn't heard her.

"See, I was arguing with logic, when what you were feeling was illogical—even to you. All you knew was that the magic had worked, whether you believed it was real or not." He turned to a young man standing several feet away, who was taking the entire scene in with undivided attention and fascination. "There's a box out in the hall. Would you bring it in for me please?"

"Payton—"

"No. No. You had your say back on the island. Now it's your turn to listen to me," he said, cutting her off as he pulled the ties of his great cape, releasing it, tossing it onto a worktable.

When his new assistant went through the door into the hall, Payton noticed several people standing in the doorway watching. He'd already met several of them.

"Come in. Join us," he said, his smile charming.

Harriet glanced to see several of her colleagues, a

few more students, the head of the science department, and the college president enter the room, their expressions passive, intrigued. Her shoulders drooped in resignation as she envisioned her dismissal.

A tall black-lacquered box with painted red flames on the sides, set on a wheeled platform, was pushed into the room and Payton picked up where he'd left off.

"My mistake was trying to argue with logic. So I went out and got some magic of my own to argue with."

"But—"

"Pay attention. A show like this is a once-in-a-lifetime deal. If you ever drive me this crazy again, I won't be held responsible for my actions," he said. Dead serious.

She couldn't stop the laugh that escaped her, and he grinned at her, loving and gentle.

With an air of mystery, he opened three small doors that formed one wall of the box. He knocked on the three remaining sides and invited Mrs. Packard, a middle-aged chemistry teacher, to inspect the box. When she was satisfied, he turned the box around once, showing it from all sides, talking magical gibberish all the while.

"If you will assist me, Ms. Wheaton," he said, holding his hand out invitingly.

Well, she couldn't beat him, because she didn't want to. So she joined him. She stepped forward and placed her hand in his. He looked at it for a second or two, gave it a soft squeeze, then brought it to his lips for a tender kiss.

"Okay," he said, all business again. "I'll just step inside here. . . ."

He did, instructing Harriet to close all the little

doors and latch them securely. This done, there soon came a muffled command for her to reopen the upper door.

"There," he said. "Now we can all see one another, and I'll amaze you with my skill." He grinned. "Harriet, please open the bottom door."

She did, revealing the lower part of his body from midcalf down. He even shuffled his feet for them, though no one was particularly impressed to see his feet at the bottom of the box.

"Are my feet still there?" he asked, craning his neck to see, as if he were surprised that they hadn't disappeared. A sympathetic group nodded at him, equally as embarrassed as he that his trick hadn't worked. He looked desperate. "Well, is the rest of me still there?"

Harriet opened the middle door. Low and behold! he was missing from neck to knee—and now he was grinning.

"Thank you, thank you," he said, nodding his decapitated head with mock humility.

Laughter rose up inside of her, and she could feel herself stepping off the deep end of sanity.

"Payton, this is truly wonderful. I'm very impressed," she said. "And I've never loved you more than I do at this minute."

"Close the doors, Harri. I want to kiss you."

She considered it, then decided, "No. I think I'll leave you there awhile longer. You see, this is a trick, a fine trick this time, but a trick nevertheless. It's not magic. It's a clever illusion. Our love is no illusion."

"I know that," he said, as if she'd called him stupid. He began to struggle a bit inside the box, though the only way she could tell was by sound. His head remained immobile, as scuffing and scraping noises came from within the box. "That's the point of all this."

"But I never claimed that the island's magic was an illusion. It's a very real thing."

"Yeah, yeah. I figured that out too," he said, the strain of his struggle showing on his face. "Now you'll get into all that supernatural stuff, like voodoo and witches, and I'm prepared for that argument too, Harri. Help me out and I'll show you."

She closed the bottom door and then stood up on her toes to talk to him. "If I close this middle one will you be able to get out easier?"

"Lord, I hope so," he said, looking pained. "I obviously can't do it with the door open, so maybe it needs to be closed."

She debated helping him a few seconds longer. It wouldn't be every day that she'd have him at so nice a disadvantage. She grinned.

"Harriet! Close the damned door. My legs are cramping."

"Will you admit that the island has a magic power?"

"No."

"Will you admit that you're acting under the influence of something you can't control?"

"Yes. But it isn't magic."

"Neither is this," she said, motioning to the box.

"Aw, Lord." He grimaced. "Please, Harri. Trip the blind, the trapdoor. Please."

Quickly she closed and latched the little door.

"What about this one?" she asked, her hand on the top door, ready to close it and end his pain.

"No." He groaned, wincing. "It's okay."

She stepped back, anxious to see if he could extricate himself from the box. A visible wave of relief passed across his face as he muttered, "Open the doors please."

The bottom door revealed his feet as before, but the middle space now contained another set of his feet—his real feet, his bent legs, and the rest of his torso. He tried to step out of the box, but his muscles were in spasm, and he sank to the floor. Harriet knelt beside him.

He closed his eyes against the pin-pricking sensation rushing through his legs as blood returned to the lower part of his body. He opened them to Harriet's face, and without a moment's hesitation, he took it between his hands and covered her mouth with his own.

The world closed in about them. The students, the department head, the other teachers, the unhatched eggs . . . they didn't exist. It was only Payton and Harriet, in love and living in a world of their own making.

"If you want this to be magic," he said, barely moving his lips from hers. "That's fine by me. I'll believe it's anything you want me to believe it is." He reached inside his shirt with one hand. "I got these amulet things from a witch in New York and the crystals from a psychic in Tampa. This . . ." he looked down then, at a small vial on a chain with yellow fluid in it. "And this, if I can get you to drink it, is a love potion I got from a very strange woman in the Everglades, guaranteed to make you love me back."

"I do love you back."

"I'll believe it's this kind of magic if you want me to, Harri. I'll hum and meditate and shave my head if that's what you want. But if you want to know my honest thoughts on it, I have to tell you that I still don't think it's magic."

She didn't care what it was anymore. All she knew, all she ever wanted to know was that she loved him and he loved her. Nothing else really mattered.

"So? What do you think it is?" she asked quietly, expecting him to say that it was love, plain and simple. An uncontrollable force with its own power, its own magic, generated not in the supernatural but on common ground between two very ordinary human beings.

"That you could possibly love me enough to make me love you. . . . Well, frankly," he said, kissing her gently, "I think it's nothing less than a miracle."

A Short Epilogue

"Ladies and gentlemen, the tale is true and in just a few moments you'll be able to see the island and decide for yourselves whether it was magic or a miracle that brought Harriet and Payton together so long ago," the automated tour guide said. She was a female model, QXM III, blond and soft-spoken, programmed to sound enthusiastic and sincere.

The hydrofoil skimmed over the water, passing between the mainland and Cedar Island toward the major traffic lanes of the antiquated but still functional waterway of the St. Lawrence River.

The group of tourists released a mass sigh of admiration as they approached another island, a mile long and forty acres wide, its slopes thickly quilled with pines and hardwoods. It boasted a prime example of nineteenth century Victorian architecture in dark olive-green, trimmed in gold and terra-cotta on the bargeboards, scalloped friezes, and porch brackets, with just a touch of Indian red here and there for accent.

"The island was officially renamed Miracle Island in the late twentieth century, several years after Harriet Jovette Wheaton married Payton Dunsmore. The island is still part of the vast Dunsmore estate and remains a favored summer residence for the family—the great-grandchildren of Payton and Harriet Dunsmore."

THE EDITOR'S CORNER

There's no better way to get into the springtime mood than to read the six fabulous LOVESWEPTs coming your way. Humorous and serious, sexy and tender, with heroes and heroines you'll long remember, these novels are guaranteed to turn May into a merry month indeed.

Leading this great lineup is Linda Jenkins with **TALL ORDER**, LOVESWEPT #612. At 6′7″, Gray Kincaid is certainly one long, tall hunk, just the kind of man statuesque Garnet Brindisi has been waiting for. And with her flamboyant, feisty manner, she's just the one-woman heat wave who can finally melt the cool reserve of the ex-basketball star called the Iceman. . . . Linda's writing makes the courtship between this unlikely couple a very exciting one to follow.

Please welcome Janis Reams Hudson, bestselling and award-winning author of historical and contemporary romances, and her first LOVESWEPT, **TRUTH OR DARE**, #613. In this touching story, Rachel Fredrick dons a shapeless dress, wig, and glasses, convinced the disguise will forever hide her real identity—and notorious past. She doesn't count on her boss, Jared Morgan, discovering the truth and daring her to let him heal her pain. Enjoy one of New Faces of '93!

STROKE BY STROKE, LOVESWEPT #614 by Patt Bucheister, is how Turner Knight wants to convince Emma Valerian she's the only woman for him. For two years she's been the best paralegal Turner has ever worked with—but the way his body heats up whenever she walks into his office has nothing to do with business. Now she's quitting and Turner can at last confess his hunger and desire. We know you'll treasure this stirring romance from Patt.

In her new LOVESWEPT, Diane Pershing gives you a dangerously sexy hero who offers nothing but **SATISFACTION**, #615. An irresistibly wicked rebel, T. R. is every woman's dream, but Kate O'Brien has vowed never to fall for another heartbreaker. Still, how can she resist a man who warns her she'll be bored with a safe, predictable guy, then dares her to play with his fire? Diane tells this story with breathtaking passion.

Prepare to thrill to romance as you read Linda Warren's second LOVESWEPT, **SWEPT AWAY**, #616. Jake Marlow never intended to return to the family whale-watching business, but he smells sabotage in the air—and he has to consider every possible suspect, including Maria Santos, the exquisitely beautiful fleet manager. The sparks of desire between these two can probably set fire to the ocean! A powerful romance from a powerful storyteller.

Adrienne Staff returns to LOVESWEPT with **PLEASURE IN THE SAND**, #617. In this heart-stirring romance, Jody Conners's nightmare of getting lost at sea turns into a dream when she's rescued by movie star Eric Ransom. Years ago Hollywood's gorgeous bad boy had suddenly dropped out of the public eye, and when he takes Jody to his private island, she discovers only she has the power to coax him—and his guarded heart—out of hiding. Welcome back, Adrienne!

On sale this month from Bantam are three fabulous novels. Teresa Medeiros follows her bestselling **HEATHER**

AND VELVET with **ONCE AN ANGEL**, a captivating historical romance that sweeps from the wilds of an exotic paradise to the elegance of Victorian England. Emily Claire Scarborough sails halfway around the world to find Justin Connor, the man who had cheated her out of her inheritance—and is determined to make him pay with nothing less than his heart.

With **IN A ROGUE'S ARMS**, Virginia Lynn delivers an enchanting, passion-filled retelling of the beloved Robin Hood tale, set in Texas in the 1870s. When Cale Hardin robs Chloe Mitchell's carriage, she swears to take revenge . . . even as she finds herself succumbing to the fascination of this bold and brazen outlaw.

IN A ROGUE'S ARMS is the first book in Bantam's ONCE UPON A TIME romances—passionate historical romances inspired by beloved fairy tales, myths, and legends, penned by some of the finest romance authors writing today, and featuring the most beautiful front and stepback covers. Be sure to look for **PROMISE ME MAGIC** by Patricia Camden, inspired by "Puss in Boots," coming in the summer of 1993, and **CAPTURE THE NIGHT** by Geralyn Dawson, inspired by "Beauty and the Beast," coming in the late fall of 1993.

Favorite LOVESWEPT author Fran Baker makes a spectacular debut in FANFARE with **THE LADY AND THE CHAMP**, which Julie Garwood has already praised as "Unforgettable . . . a warm, wonderful knockout of a book." You'll cheer as Maureen Bryant and Jack Ryan risk anything—even Jack's high-stakes return to the ring—to fight for their chance at love.

Bantam/Doubleday/Dell welcomes Jane Feather with the Doubleday hardcover edition of **VIRTUE**. Set in Regency England, this highly sensual tale brings together a strong-willed beauty who makes her living at the gaming tables and the arrogant nobleman determined to best her with passion.

Happy reading!

With warmest wishes,

Nita Taublib
Associate Publisher
LOVESWEPT and FANFARE

OFFICIAL RULES TO WINNERS CLASSIC SWEEPSTAKES

No Purchase necessary. To enter the sweepstakes follow instructions found elsewhere in this offer. You can also enter the sweepstakes by hand printing your name, address, city, state and zip code on a 3" x 5" piece of paper and mailing it to: Winners Classic Sweepstakes, P.O. Box 785, Gibbstown, NJ 08027. Mail each entry separately. Sweepstakes begins 12/1/91. Entries must be received by 6/1/93. Some presentations of this sweepstakes may feature a deadline for the Early Bird prize. If the offer you receive does, then to be eligible for the Early Bird prize your entry must be received according to the Early Bird date specified. Not responsible for lost, late, damaged, misdirected, illegible or postage due mail. Mechanically reproduced entries are not eligible. All entries become property of the sponsor and will not be returned.

Prize Selection/Validations: Winners will be selected in random drawings on or about 7/30/93, by VENTURA ASSOCIATES, INC., an independent judging organization whose decisions are final. Odds of winning are determined by total number of entries received. Circulation of this sweepstakes is estimated not to exceed 200 million. Entrants need not be present to win. All prizes are guaranteed to be awarded and delivered to winners. Winners will be notified by mail and may be required to complete an affidavit of eligibility and release of liability which must be returned within 14 days of date of notification or alternate winners will be selected. Any guest of a trip winner will also be required to execute a release of liability. Any prize notification letter or any prize returned to a participating sponsor, Bantam Doubleday Dell Publishing Group, Inc., its participating divisions or subsidiaries, or VENTURA ASSOCIATES, INC. as undeliverable will be awarded to an alternate winner. Prizes are not transferable. No multiple prize winners except as may be necessary due to unavailability, in which case a prize of equal or greater value will be awarded. Prizes will be awarded approximately 90 days after the drawing. All taxes, automobile license and registration fees, if applicable, are the sole responsibility of the winners. Entry constitutes permission (except where prohibited) to use winners' names and likenesses for publicity purposes without further or other compensation.

Participation: This sweepstakes is open to residents of the United States and Canada, except for the province of Quebec. This sweepstakes is sponsored by Bantam Doubleday Dell Publishing Group, Inc. (BDD), 666 Fifth Avenue, New York, NY 10103. Versions of this sweepstakes with different graphics will be offered in conjunction with various solicitations or promotions by different subsidiaries and divisions of BDD. Employees and their families of BDD, its division, subsidiaries, advertising agencies, and VENTURA ASSOCIATES, INC., are not eligible.

Canadian residents, in order to win, must first correctly answer a time limited arithmetical skill testing question. Void in Quebec and wherever prohibited or restricted by law. Subject to all federal, state, local and provincial laws and regulations.

Prizes: The following values for prizes are determined by the manufacturers' suggested retail prices or by what these items are currently known to be selling for at the time this offer was published. Approximate retail values include handling and delivery of prizes. Estimated maximum retail value of prizes: 1 Grand Prize ($27,500 if merchandise or $25,000 Cash); 1 First Prize ($3,000); 5 Second Prizes ($400 each); 35 Third Prizes ($100 each); 1,000 Fourth Prizes ($9.00 each); 1 Early Bird Prize ($5,000); Total approximate maximum retail value is $50,000. Winners will have the option of selecting any prize offered at level won. Automobile winner must have a valid driver's license at the time the car is awarded. Trips are subject to space and departure availability. Certain black-out dates may apply. Travel must be completed within one year from the time the prize is awarded. Minors must be accompanied by an adult. Prizes won by minors will be awarded in the name of parent or legal guardian.

For a list of Major Prize Winners (available after 7/30/93): send a self-addressed, stamped envelope entirely separate from your entry to: Winners Classic Sweepstakes Winners, P.O. Box 825, Gibbstown, NJ 08027. Requests must be received by 6/1/93. DO NOT SEND ANY OTHER CORRESPONDENCE TO THIS P.O. BOX.

SWP 9/92